P9-CDX-666

"Can I ask you a personal question?"

When Mike didn't immediately shake his head, Melanie went on. "Brenda's an attractive woman and she seems nice enough. Why aren't you interested?"

"My life's complicated enough. I'm not looking for a relationship."

Melanie could relate to that. "And I imagine it's a whole lot easier to give a rosebush what it needs than it is to deal with a woman."

His lips quirked slightly. "Couldn't have said it better myself."

Even though she could relate all too well to where he was coming from, some traitorous little voice deep inside her couldn't help murmuring, "Lucky rosebush."

Mike regarded her oddly. "What was that?"

Oh, Lord, had she really said that out loud?

Dear Reader,

Spring might be just around the corner, but it's not too late to curl up by the fire with this month's lineup of six heartwarming stories. Start off with *Three Down the Aisle*, the first book in bestselling author Sherryl Woods's new miniseries, THE ROSE COTTAGE SISTERS. When a woman returns to her childhood haven, the last thing she expects is to fall in love! And make sure to come back in April for the next book in this delightful new series.

Will a sexy single dad find *All He Ever Wanted* in a search-and-rescue worker who saves his son? Find out in Allison Leigh's latest book in our MONTANA MAVERICKS: GOLD RUSH GROOMS miniseries. The Fortunes of Texas are back, and you can read the first three stories in the brand-new miniseries THE FORTUNES OF TEXAS: REUNION, only in Silhouette Special Edition. The continuity launches with *Her Good Fortune* by Marie Ferrarella. Can a straitlaced CEO make it work with a feisty country girl who's taken the big city by storm? Next, don't miss the latest book in Susan Mallery's DESERT ROGUES ongoing miniseries, *The Sheik & the Bride Who Said No*. When two former lovers reunite, passion flares again. But can they forgive each other for past mistakes? Be sure to read the next book in Judy Duarte's miniseries, BAYSIDE BACHELORS. A fireman discovers his ex-lover's child is *Their Secret Son*, but can they be a family once again? And pick up Crystal Green's *The Millionaire's Secret Baby*. When a ranch chef lands her childhood crush—and tycoon—can she keep her identity hidden, or will he discover her secrets?

Enjoy, and be sure to come back next month for six compelling new novels, from Silhouette Special Edition.

All the best,

Gail Chasan
Senior Editor

Please address questions and book requests to:
Silhouette Reader Service
U.S.: 3010 Walden Ave., P.O. Box 1325, Buffalo, NY 14269
Canadian: P.O. Box 609, Fort Erie, Ont. L2A 5X3

SHERRYL WOODS

Three Down the Aisle

Silhouette

SPECIAL EDITION

Published by Silhouette Books

America's Publisher of Contemporary Romance

If you purchased this book without a cover you should be aware
that this book is stolen property. It was reported as "unsold and
destroyed" to the publisher, and neither the author nor the
publisher has received any payment for this "stripped book."

SILHOUETTE BOOKS

ISBN 0-373-24663-3

THREE DOWN THE AISLE

Copyright © 2005 by Sherryl Woods

All rights reserved. Except for use in any review, the reproduction
or utilization of this work in whole or in part in any form by any
electronic, mechanical or other means, now known or hereafter
invented, including xerography, photocopying and recording, or in
any information storage or retrieval system, is forbidden without
the written permission of the editorial office, Silhouette Books,
233 Broadway, New York, NY 10279 U.S.A.

All characters in this book have no existence outside the imagination of
the author and have no relation whatsoever to anyone bearing the same
name or names. They are not even distantly inspired by any individual
known or unknown to the author, and all incidents are pure invention.

This edition published by arrangement with Harlequin Books S.A.

® and TM are trademarks of Harlequin Books S.A., used under license.
Trademarks indicated with ® are registered in the United States Patent
and Trademark Office, the Canadian Trade Marks Office and in other
countries.

Visit Silhouette Books at www.eHarlequin.com

Printed in U.S.A.

Books by Sherryl Woods

SHERRYL WOODS

has written more than seventy-five novels. She also operates her own bookstore, Potomac Sunrise, in Colonial Beach, Virginia. If you can't visit Sherryl at her store, then be sure to drop her a note at P.O. Box 490326, Key Biscayne, FL 33149 or check out her Web site at www.sherrylwoods.com.

Dear Reader,

All of us have someplace in our lives that we remember fondly. Sometimes it's only nostalgia that colors a perfectly ordinary place and lifts it into a special place in our hearts. Sometimes it's a place that truly was magical during our childhoods. For me that was always the family cottage by the Potomac River.

Now that I'm living part of the year back in my very special place, it got me thinking about what would happen to four sisters as each of them faced a turning point in their lives. What if they had spent their summers in a cottage that held a special place in their hearts? Would they retreat there to heal? And would that serene place once more open their hearts to the possibility of love? And so, I began to write about the Rose Cottage Sisters, four wonderful, strong women in search of peace.

In *Three Down the Aisle,* you'll meet Melanie D'Angelo who, frankly, is not all that overjoyed about being banished to the shores of the Chesapeake Bay when a romance blows up in her face. She wants nothing more than to hide out until the shame and embarrassment of her broken love affair die down.

But Rose Cottage is in need of some serious attention when she arrives and sexy landscape designer Stefan Mikelewski has a few ideas about where she ought to begin. For a man of few words, Mike has a lot to say about the sorry state of her grandmother's garden. His loving attention to the roses and his nurturing devotion to his troubled six-year-old provide a healing balm for Melanie, as well. And, before she knows it, love is blooming right alongside those beautiful heirloom roses.

I hope you enjoy Melanie and Mike's story and that you'll share just a little of the magic of Rose Cottage.

All best,

Sheryl Woods

Prologue

The tears on her cheeks were still damp and her temper was still hot, when someone—no, not just someone, the family calvary—pounded on the door of Melanie's Boston apartment. Before she could drag herself off the sofa, the door burst open and all three of her sisters swooped into her tiny studio looking a bit like outraged avenging angels.

If Melanie hadn't been so completely and totally miserable and humiliated, she might have managed to smile at their ready-for-anything attitude. Had her sisters gotten here before she'd kicked Jeremy the weasel to the curb, he'd probably be quaking in his two-hundred-dollar designer loafers.

The D'Angelo sisters were something else. Singly, they had their own distinctive personalities and achievements, but united they were a force to be reckoned with. And nothing united them like a common enemy—in this case the man who'd lied to Melanie for more than six months.

Maggie and Jo settled on either side of her, patting her hands and murmuring inept but well-meant platitudes about how things would improve, how she was better off without the lying, cheating scoundrel and on and on until Melanie wanted to scream.

Ashley, she noticed, was saying nothing, but her agitated pacing and the flags of color on her cheeks suggested that an explosion was in the offing. Ashley took her duties as the oldest and most successful of the D'Angelo sisters seriously. She also had their father's volatile temper. Melanie eyed her warily.

"Ash, maybe you should sit down," she suggested quietly. "You're giving us all whiplash trying to follow you."

Her big sister responded with a frown. "I don't think so. I'm trying to decide whether to haul this Jeremy's sorry butt into court or just hunt him down and pound him to a pulp."

The rest of the sisters exchanged a look. With Ashley, neither option was entirely out of the question. She had a law degree, a powerful sense of justice, a protective streak and a right hook that deserved respect.

"What good would any of that do, Ash?" Jo the peacemaker inquired cautiously. "Getting your name splashed in the papers along with the whole tawdry reason for your behavior would only prolong Melanie's pain and humiliate her in front of the entire world. Then everyone would know that the creep pulled the wool over her eyes for months. Do you actually want Dad to find out about this? You'll be in court defending him on a murder charge."

Ashley sighed. "True."

They all fell silent, considering Jo's warning. Their father was a lusty, boisterous Italian who'd put the fear of God into more of their dates than any of them cared to recall. And those were the *nice* guys. Jeremy the weasel wouldn't stand a chance against their father's outrage.

Ashley peered intently at Melanie. "Are you sure you don't want me to do something? There are lots of ways to get even that don't involve bloodshed."

"Nothing," Melanie assured her hurriedly. "It's bad enough that you all know that Jeremy managed to hide a wife and two kids from me, that I believed him every single time he evaded my questions about why we couldn't see each other on the weekends, why we spent so little time in public. He made it all sound perfectly reasonable."

"What made him get around to telling you tonight? A guilty conscience?" Maggie asked.

"Hardly," Melanie admitted. "I ran smack into him while they were all out buying new sneakers for the kids. Even then, he tried to drag me out of sight and tell me some lie about how he was just being dutiful, that it didn't mean a thing, that the marriage was on its last legs. Blah, blah, blah. Idiot that I am, I probably would have listened, too, if his wife hadn't seen us and given him a look that would have frozen anyone else on the spot. Something tells me that this isn't the first time Jeremy's been caught straying by his wife. Her radar was on full alert. How he managed to get away from her to come over here to try one more time to explain is beyond me."

"You didn't listen to a word he had to say, did you?" Ashley demanded.

"Of course not. By then you all were on your way. I

wanted him long gone when you got here.'' She sighed. ''How stupid was I? I should have done the math on this months ago.''

Jo grinned as she nudged Melanie in the ribs. ''You always were lousy at math.''

''Not funny, baby sister,'' Melanie retorted. ''What am I going to do now? I certainly can't continue working at Rockingham Industries. If this isn't proof that you should never get involved with someone at the same company—even a company as huge as Rockingham—I don't know what is. My stomach twists into a knot just at the thought of seeing him again. And to think that only a day ago, I did everything I could to bump into him in the hallways.''

''You need to get away, take some time off,'' Maggie said, her expression thoughtful. ''And I know the perfect place.''

''I need to get another job,'' Melanie corrected. ''I know I wasn't exactly on the fast track at Rockingham, but that receptionist's job did pay the rent.''

''You don't need to look right away,'' Ashley insisted. ''If you're short on cash, I can lend you whatever you need.''

''Says the high-powered criminal defense attorney who's rolling in dough and has no time to spend it,'' Jo said. ''The rest of us will chip in, too.''

''Agreed,'' Maggie said at once.

Ashley nodded. ''There, that's taken care of. And I think I see exactly where Maggie was going a minute ago. You should go to Grandma's cottage, Melanie. We always thought it was magical there. I can't imagine a more perfect place to get your head on straight.''

''We were kids,'' Melanie pointed out. ''It was summer vacation. *Of course* we thought it was magical. Notice that none of us has been back since we grew up. Not even Mom goes down anymore, now that Grandma's dead. The place is probably a wreck.''

"All the more reason to go," Ashley said, obviously warming to Maggie's idea. "Fixing up the cottage will be just what you need. It's probably worth a fortune. If no one's ever going to use it, maybe we can talk Mom into selling."

"She'll never do it," Maggie said. "You know how sentimental she is about that place."

Ashley waved off the comment. "Beside the point."

"What is the point?" Jo asked. "I'm losing track."

"Fixing the house up will keep Melanie's mind occupied all day, and by night she'll be so exhausted, she'll fall right to sleep," Ashley explained. "The rest of us can take turns going down weekends to keep her company."

"Am I such an embarrassment that you can't wait to get rid of me?" Melanie asked plaintively.

She wasn't sure she wanted to go away someplace where she'd be all alone with only her thoughts for company. Grandma's place, Rose Cottage, was on the banks of the Chesapeake Bay at the tip of Virginia's Northern Neck. With the recent growth of the region, she doubted it was as isolated and tranquil as it had once been, but by Boston standards it was still rural. She doubted there was a movie theater or a mall for miles, much less a Starbucks.

"This isn't a banishment," Ashley insisted.

"But why should I give Jeremy the satisfaction of running away?" Melanie argued. "He's the scumbag."

"She has a point," Jo said.

Ashley scowled at both of them. "So, what are you suggesting? You'll face him down every morning when he walks in the front door at Rockingham? That sounds like fun.''

Actually it sounded like hell, Melanie was forced to admit.

"Come on, Melanie. You know I'm right," Ashley persisted. "This is a chance to heal. You'll have time to decide what you want to do next. It's about time you put that college degree of yours to use. You were wasting your talent at Rockingham on the off chance that someday there would be an opening in the marketing department. This could be the best thing that ever happened to you, if it finally gets you to find the right job, instead of something safe but boring."

At the moment, with her heart aching and her pride wounded, Melanie couldn't quite see tonight's turn of events as any sort of blessing, but Ashley usually knew best. "If you say so," she said bleakly.

"Would you rather sit in this apartment and mope?" Ashley demanded.

"No," Melanie said firmly. She'd never moped in her life, and she didn't intend to start now, not over the likes of Jeremy Thompson of the Providence and Nantucket Thompsons. How had she let herself be fooled by that impeccable breeding? Charm and a pedigree didn't mean a man had character.

"Good. That's settled, then," Ashley said. "We'll help you pack. You can leave first thing in the morning. It's a long drive, and you'll want to get there while it's still daylight."

"I haven't even turned in my resignation at work," Melanie protested. Not that she had any great desire to show her face around there as long as there was any chance at all she could bump into Jeremy.

"Fax it in," Ashley said curtly. "If anyone questions

it, tell them to take it up with Jeremy. Let him explain. Maybe they'll fire his sorry butt. Or, have them call me, and I'll explain a few facts about sexual harassment.''

"It wasn't—" Melanie began, only to have her big sister cut her off.

"It was close enough," Ashley said. "He dangled the prospect of a better job in front of you, didn't he?''

"Yes," Melanie admitted. Even so, despite the appeal of a little vengeance, she still wasn't entirely convinced. They'd all been brought up with a strong sense of duty and responsibility. Responsible people gave two weeks' notice before walking out on a job, even a job they hated, even a job that clearly had never had any future. Surely her sisters had learned that lesson, too.

"But—" she began.

"No buts," Ashley said firmly.

Melanie sighed. "Okay, then. How am I supposed to get the key from Mom without telling her the whole ugly story?" she asked, grabbing at straws to keep from facing the inevitability of this trip. Their mother, to all outward appearances, might be a gentle southern belle, but she had the same kind of iron will their father had. She was every bit as capable as Max D'Angelo of making Jeremy's life hell. She'd been inspired by *Gone with the Wind,* so much so that three of her four daughters had been named after characters and the author. Only Jo had escaped that fate. They teased Jo all the time that it was only because their mother has secretly thought of herself as Scarlett.

"Don't worry about Mom." Ashley dug into her huge purse and pulled out an old-fashioned key attached to a piece of rose-colored satin ribbon. "I keep a spare in my purse," she said, looking vaguely embarrassed.

Melanie, Jo and Maggie stared at her. "Why?"

"It's like a talisman," she said defensively. "Whenever things get really, really crazy and frantic at work, I take it out and remind myself that there *is* life after court. There are days when *I* would go to Rose Cottage if I could."

"But you haven't been there in years," Melanie said, bemused by this rare display of sentiment and frivolity in her hard-as-nails big sister.

Ashley winked. "Obviously just knowing it's there works like a charm."

Melanie sighed. If only the cottage would hold a few of those magical healing properties for her, she'd be eternally grateful. Right now, with the image of those kids and his wife's icy disdain in her head and Jeremy's stinging admission still ringing in her ears, she had her doubts.

Chapter One

Every morning when Mike drove his daughter to school past the old Lindsey cottage, he bit back a sigh of regret over its decrepit state. It was like a neglected doll's cottage, abandoned by a fickle child who'd moved on to other toys. The screens on the side porch had been torn by vandals, the front steps sagged, the paint was peeling. One dangling shutter slapped against the side of the house whenever there was any sort of breeze.

The house sat on a valuable piece of property that backed up to the Chesapeake Bay. From the road, the view was all but invisible thanks to the overgrown grass and shrubbery, but it had to be incredible. That anyone could abandon such a place and leave it to the elements to be destroyed was a crime. If they weren't going to use it, they should sell to someone who'd take proper care of it.

But if the sorry state of the house bothered Mike, it

was the garden that made him want to leap from the car with his pruning shears, rakes and shovels. Landscape design was his passion, and he could tell that once upon a time, this place had been a garden showcase. Someone had nurtured the roses that struggled to bloom there now. Someone had given thought to the placement of the lilacs right beneath the windows where the fragrance would drift in on a spring morning.

Now, though, the roses were out of control, tangled with thorny vines. Honeysuckle had taken over the lilacs. The paint on the picket fence was peeling, and parts of it were close to collapse under the weight of the untamed bushes. A few perennials continued to struggle against the weeds, but the weeds were winning. It made him heartsick to see it all gone to ruin.

He'd wanted to buy it himself at first sight six years ago, but the real estate agent said the owner wasn't interested in selling. Apparently the owner wasn't interested in anything having to do with the house, either.

"Daddy," Jessie piped up from beside him. "Why are we stopping here? This place is scary."

Mike glanced over at his six-year-old daughter, who, at the moment, looked like a Victorian painting of a blue-eyed, blond-haired angel. There were no smudges on her cheeks, no tangles in her hair, no rips in her clothes. In fact, she was having a good morning so far. There had been no tantrums over which dress to put on, no battles over the scrambled eggs he'd set in front of her for breakfast because they were out of Cheerios. Days like this were so rare, Mike had learned to cherish them when they came.

Not that he would trade one single second of the time he spent with her, tantrums or not. Jessie was his precious girl, his little survivor. She'd been through way too much in her young life. She'd been born addicted to the drugs her mother hadn't been able to quit, drugs Mike hadn't even realized Linda was hiding from him. When doctors at the hospital had told him his irritable, underweight baby girl was going through withdrawal, he'd been stunned.

He'd spent the next six months after that battling with Linda, trying to get her into rehab, trying to make her see that she was destroying not only her own life and their marriage, but their daughter's life as well. Unfortunately, nothing he'd said had gotten through to her. The drugs were far more powerful, far more alluring than his love or the needs of their baby girl.

Finally, filled with despair, he'd gone to court, gotten his divorce and full custody of Jessie, and left. Linda's folks knew where to find them, if Linda ever got her act together and wanted to see her child. Until then, though, Linda was out of their lives.

Linda's heartsick parents had agreed that he had no choice. That, at least, had given him some comfort, knowing they believed he'd done what he'd had to do. They visited regularly, but Linda's name was rarely mentioned, especially in front of Jessie. Now that she was old enough to understand, when she asked the inevitable questions about her mother, Mike answered as honestly as he could, but it broke his heart to see the hurt in Jessie's eyes.

Being a single dad would have been hard under any circumstances, but dealing with Jessie's lingering behavior problems was enough to test the patience of a saint. As a baby, she'd screamed her dissatisfaction night and day. Now she was simply unpredictable, sunny one minute and hysterical the next.

Most days Mike was up to the task of dealing with

her mood swings, but there were times when it was all he could do not to break down in exhaustion and weep for the damage that had been done to his beautiful little girl.

That was one reason he'd chosen the small town of Irvington on the Chesapeake Bay. There was plenty of work to be had here, but the pace was slower and less demanding than it would have been in a major city. If he needed to spend extra time with Jessie, he could do so without feeling he was shortchanging his clients. And, because his reputation was excellent, he could pick and choose among those who sought his services, making sure that each of them understood that Jessie would always be his first priority.

"We need to go *now!*" Jessie commanded. Even at six, she had the imperial presence of a queen commanding her subjects. She lowered her voice and confided, "I think ghosts live here, Daddy."

Mike grinned at her. It wasn't the first time she'd expressed a negative opinion about the rundown place, but the addition of a ghost was something new. "What makes you think that, pumpkin?" he asked.

"Something moved at the window. I saw it." Her lower lip trembled, and panic filled her eyes.

"Nobody lives here," Mike reassured her. "The house is empty."

"Something moved," Jessie said stubbornly, clearly near tears. Whether she'd actually seen something or not, her fear was real. "We need to *go!*"

Rather than argue, Mike accelerated and continued on to the school. Any logical response he could have made would only have escalated the tension, and the rare serenity would have been shattered.

As soon as they were away from the house, Jessie's

shoulders eased and she gave him a tremulous smile. "We're safe now," she said happily.

"You're always safe when I'm around," Mike reminded her.

"I know, Daddy," she said patiently. "But I don't like that place. I don't want to go there again. Not ever. Promise."

"We have to drive by it every day," Mike said.

"But only really, really fast," Jessie insisted. "Okay?"

Mike sighed, knowing that reasoning with his daughter when she was like this was a waste of breath. "Okay."

"Have a good day, pumpkin," he said a few minutes later when he left Jessie at the front door of the school. "I'll be right here when you get out this afternoon."

He'd discovered early on that she needed to be reassured again and again that he would be back, that he wouldn't forget about her. The psychologist he'd spoken to said Jessie's need for constant reassurance was yet another effect of not having her mother in her life, of knowing that Linda had abandoned her. Some days he wondered if he shouldn't have lied and said Linda was dead, if that wouldn't have been less cruel, but he hadn't been able to bring himself to do it. Maybe he'd naively held out hope that someday Linda would straighten herself out and want to be a part of their daughter's life.

"Bye, Daddy." Jessie turned away, then looked back at him, her expression filled with worry. "You won't go back to the bad house, will you? I don't want the ghost to get you."

"No ghost is going to get me," Mike promised, sketching a cross over his heart in the way he always did to reassure her that he meant what he said. "I wear ghost repellent."

Jessie giggled. "You're silly," she told him, though genuine relief flashed in her eyes.

Then she was gone, racing to catch up with a friend. Mike stared after her, wishing it could always be this easy to calm her fears. Some nights there was no consoling her. Some nights she had nightmares she refused to describe, calming only when he held her.

When Jessie was finally out of sight, he turned on his heel and went back to the car, already planning his jam-packed schedule for the few hours till school let out again.

But instead of heading toward the job he had land-scaping a newly completed house overlooking the bay, he drove back to the Lindsey place, drawn by something he couldn't quite explain.

Had Jessie actually seen something move? Or was he simply reacting to her too-vivid imagination, caught up in the mystery of the deserted house that had fascinated him from the moment he'd arrived in town? Whichever it was, it wouldn't take more than a few minutes to put his mind at rest and satisfy his curiosity. Maybe then he'd be able to put his mild obsession with the place behind him once and for all.

Melanie was standing in her grandmother's kitchen ineffectively battling cobwebs, when the front gate creaked, sending her already jittery nerves into a full-blown panic attack.

Only a few minutes earlier she'd thought she heard a car stop on the isolated road, but when she'd peeked through the curtain of her upstairs bedroom, she'd seen only a glimpse of sun on metal before hearing the car drive on. The incident, which would have been commonplace enough in Boston, had been oddly disconcerting here.

With her heart pumping and her pulse racing once more, she crept into the living room and edged toward the window she'd thrown open to let in the cool spring breeze.

"What the hell?"

The very male voice just outside had her plastering her back to the wall, even as her heart ricocheted wildly.

"Anybody here?" the man shouted, rattling the doorknob.

This wasn't good, not good at all, Melanie decided. Her cell phone was across the room, just more proof that she wasn't thinking clearly of late. Even with all the recent development she'd noticed as she drove in, the nearest neighbor was a quarter-mile up the road. There were a few boats on the bay this morning and sound did carry near water, but would anyone get here in time even if she shouted for help?

She tried to think what Ashley would do. Her fearless big sister would probably have a firm grip on a lamp by now and be in attack mode by the door. Picturing it, Melanie reached for the closest lamp with its heavy marble base and tested its weight. This sucker could do some real damage, she concluded, suddenly feeling more confident and in control.

"Who's there?" she shouted back in what she hoped was a suitably indignant tone. "You're trespassing."

"So are you."

She was so taken aback by the outrageous accusation that she swung open the door and scowled at the interloper. It was amazing how much braver she felt with that lamp and a little indignation on her side.

"I most certainly am not trespassing," she said again, trying not to let her voice waver at the sight of the hulking man on the threshold.

At least six-two and easily two hundred pounds, he was all muscle and sinew. Even though it was barely April, his skin had already been burnished gold by the sun, and his dark-brown hair had fiery highlights in it. His T-shirt stretched tightly over a massive chest, and his faded jeans hugged impressive thighs. An illustration of Paul Bunyon immediately came to mind.

At any other time in her life, she might have been more appreciative of such a gorgeous male specimen, but in recent days anything driven by testosterone was the enemy. That didn't seem to stop her heartbeat from skipping merrily at the sight of him. Given his obviously sour mood, her instinctive response was doubly annoying.

"Cornelia Lindsey is dead," he announced, his blue eyes steady and unrelenting as he challenged her to dispute that.

"I know," Melanie said. "She was my grandmother. She died seven years ago this month."

He nodded slowly. "You've got that much right. You're a Lindsey?"

"Actually I'm a D'Angelo. Melanie D'Angelo. My mother was a Lindsey until she married my father."

"Cornelia Lindsey was southern through and through, according to the neighbors. You don't sound like you're from around here."

"I'm not. I'm from Boston."

"You have any ID?"

She regarded him with a mix of amusement and defensiveness. "None with my family tree printed on it. Who *are* you? The local sheriff or something?"

"Just a neighbor. This place has been empty a long time. Someone turns up out of the blue like this, I just want to be sure they belong here. If you are who you say you are, I'm sure you can appreciate that."

It was evident to Melanie that he wasn't going to budge without some sort of proof that she wasn't a stranger setting up housekeeping in an abandoned property. He was right. She ought to be grateful that a neighbor would take such interest in making sure the cottage was secure.

"Stay there," she muttered, then stared at the lamp she still held clutched in her hands. She set it back on its table, then crossed the room to grab her purse and several of the framed snapshots sitting on the old oak sideboard.

When she returned, she handed him her driver's license, then a photo of a grinning girl with freckles and hair bleached almost white by the sun. "That's me at six," she said, then showed him the rest. "My sisters, Maggie, Ashley and Jo with our mom. And this one is of all of us with my grandmother, Cornelia Lindsey, just before she died. Did you know her?"

"No," he said, taking the photo and studying it intently.

To her surprise, he barely spared a glance for her sisters, all of them long-legged beauties. Instead, his gaze seemed to be focused on something else in the picture.

"I knew it," he mumbled, then scowled at her. "You all should be ashamed of yourselves."

She flinched at the outrage in his tone. "I beg your pardon!"

"The garden," he said impatiently. "You've let it go to ruin."

Melanie sighed. She could hardly deny it was a disgrace. She'd all but had to chop her way through it to get inside. She was pretty sure her car was likely to be swallowed up by aggressive vines if she didn't move it on a regular basis.

"I noticed," she conceded mildly.

His frown deepened. "Now that you're here, what do you intend to do about it?"

Melanie shrugged. She could have told him it was none of his business, but she didn't have the energy to argue about something so unimportant with a total stranger. Nor was she inclined to defend their neglect of the house or the garden. It really was indefensible, given the way their grandmother had loved this house and doted on her roses.

"I don't know," she said eventually. "Something, I suppose. First, though, I have to air this place out and chase out seven years' worth of spiders and bug carcasses."

The man on her doorstep regarded her with undisguised disapproval. "Don't wait too long. Now is the time of year to fix it." He dug in his pocket and handed her a card. "When you're ready, call me. It needs to be done right, and something tells me you've never gotten your hands dirty." He shot a disdainful glance toward her pale, smooth hands. "I'll show you what to do, so you don't make things worse than they already are."

Before she could reject the ungracious offer, before she could even muster a suitably indignant retort, he'd turned on his heel and gone, crashing through the overgrown weeds and vines like an intrepid explorer in alien jungle territory. He stopped several times to examine the rosebushes with a surprisingly gentle caress or to tug violently at a choking strand of honeysuckle, muttering to himself in an undertone. Melanie had little doubt that whatever he was saying was unflattering.

Annoyed by his judgmental attitude, she was about to rip the card to shreds, but something about the delicate artwork in one corner caught her eye. It was only a line drawing, but the combination of seagrass and roses reminded her of the way Rose Cottage had been in its heyday. He was right about one thing. Her grandmother would be appalled by the garden's sorry state of neglect.

Her gaze moved from the drawing to the name.

Stefan Mikelewski, Landscape Designer, the card said simply, along with a phone number.

Okay, so he was abrupt and abrasive, but he apparently had actual expertise she could use if she was to make any headway at all in the disastrous garden. She tucked the card in her pocket, then went back to the kitchen, hoping to brew a cup of tea so she could start the day all over again.

One look around, though, told her that even the simple task of boiling water was entirely too daunting to contemplate on an empty stomach. It could take hours to get the stove clean enough to set a teakettle on one of the burners. Coffee was out of the question with no sign of a coffee grinder for the special-blend beans she'd brought with her. Maggie, with her gourmet mentality, had instilled a love of perfect coffee, along with a taste for haute cuisine, in all of the sisters.

Melanie consoled herself that she wasn't really running away from all the work that needed to be done. She had to go into town anyway so she could stock the refrigerator with groceries and spend a fortune on cleaning supplies. The fast-food dinner she'd had before she'd arrived the night before had worn off hours ago, and she was definitely going to need stamina to tackle the thorough cleaning the house required. Last night she'd done little more than sweep out the attic bedroom she and her sisters had always used and make up the bed with the fresh sheets she'd brought with her.

Turning her back on the mess was perfectly sensible, she concluded. "It'll be just as much of a disaster when I get back," she told herself, grabbing her purse and heading for the door.

In fact, something told her she could spend the next week scrubbing the place from top to bottom and she'd barely make a dent in the cleanup effort. As much as she'd hated Jeremy a scant thirty-six hours ago, her sisters were about to join him on the shortlist of people Melanie didn't want to see anytime soon, not unless they came wielding dust rags and brooms.

Her cell phone rang just as she pulled into a parking space in Irvington's small downtown district, where she'd noticed a promising coffee shop the night before.

"Relaxing yet?" Ashley inquired cheerily.

"Remember what you said about being so exhausted from cleaning I wouldn't have time to think?" Melanie muttered. "It took two hours to clear a path to the bed last night."

"Uh-oh," her sister responded.

"Triple whatever image you have in your mind, and you'll have some idea of the work ahead of me. And that's inside. The yard's worse."

"That bad?"

"And then some."

"How's the weather?"

"Don't change the subject. I want you to know just how annoyed I am with all of you right now. I feel like Cinderella, left behind to deal with the mess her wicked stepsisters didn't want to touch."

"Hey, it sounds like this is working out just fine," Ashley countered.

"In whose universe?" Melanie retorted.

"You're not thinking about Jeremy, are you?" Ashley said. "Gotta run. I'm due in court. Love you."

Melanie tossed her cell phone back in her purse. Much as she hated to admit it, her sister was right. She hadn't thought about Jeremy the scumbag all morning, except in passing. Whether that was due to the daunting prospect of cleaning Rose Cottage or the equally daunting encounter with Stefan Mikelewski was hard to say.

"Blame it on the cleaning," she muttered to herself as she headed for a coffee shop down the block. Thinking about doing battle with dust bunnies was a whole lot safer than remembering the way the landscaper had made her blood hum through her veins, especially when he'd deliberately taunted her about the condition of the garden. Maybe that was a reaction to his arrogance and nothing more, but she didn't want to test the theory with another encounter anytime soon.

As she drank her coffee and ate an entire huge cinnamon roll, she considered how fortunate it was that she had days and days of work ahead of her inside the house before she could even begin to contemplate doing anything outside. That would give her time to decide if she wanted to tackle it on her own or ask for help from the disconcerting Mr. Mikelewski.

Or maybe just hightail it back to Boston and forget the whole thing.

Now there was an idea, she thought happily—until she remembered the reason she'd left in the first place. She swallowed hard and steeled her resolve to stay right here.

After all, no amount of dirt and grime, no tangle of weeds, no judgmental scowls from Mr. Mikelewski could be awful enough to drive her back to the city where Jeremy was contentedly living with the wife and two children he'd neglected to mention to her until she'd caught him red-handed.

The memory of her total humiliation was a terrific motivator, she concluded, as she made a whirlwind trip through the grocery store and exited with a cart piled high with comfort food and antibacterial scrubbing supplies.

She was going to wash years of dirt out of Rose Cottage and toss every last memory of Jeremy out with the filthy water…or die trying.

Chapter Two

It had been a week now, and Mike hadn't been able to shake the image of Melanie D'Angelo standing in her doorway clutching a heavy lamp and facing him down without the slightest hint of trepidation. Of course, there had been shadows in her cornflower-blue eyes and smudges on her pale cheeks, but she'd shown absolutely no fear in the face of his intrusive, skeptical questions or his condemnation of the garden's sad neglect. He'd been impressed, to say nothing of intrigued. Now, thanks to that unexpected encounter, he was more drawn to the Lindsey cottage than ever.

It was the shadows in her eyes that had gotten to him. They were evidence of the kind of vulnerability he tended to avoid like the plague these days. He had all the emotional upset in his life he could cope with. He didn't need to go taking on some stranger's woes, even if she did have skin like silk and a body that all but

begged for a man's attention. He still hadn't forgotten
the way her blouse had gaped slightly to reveal a slight
hint of cleavage or the way her jeans had clung to the
curve of her hips and her endlessly long legs.

He didn't need a woman in his life, especially not one
who all but shouted that she came with complications.

Hell, he had all the work he could handle, too. He
didn't need to go looking for any more, especially of the
unpaid variety. She hadn't called, so obviously she
didn't think she needed his help untangling that mess in
her yard. He should forget all about Melanie D'Angelo
and the Lindsey cottage. They were someone else's
problem.

But then he remembered the photo she'd shown him.
Oh, he'd noticed the four gorgeous teenagers and their
handsome mother and smiling grandmother, but his heart
had done a little stutter-step at the sight of the climbing
pink, white and red roses, the heirloom tea roses, the
brilliant orange tiger lilies, the stately hollyhocks. Someone—Cornelia Lindsey, obviously—had tended that garden with love, and it deserved respect by those who
followed. Her descendants *should* be ashamed for not
nurturing such an incredible legacy.

That was one of the things he liked most about his
work. If a man spent time nurturing a garden, planting
carefully, watering, weeding and fertilizing, he could
count on it to offer beauty and behave predictably.

Nature had its whims, of course. Hurricane Isabel in
2003 had wreaked havoc on many of the stately old trees
around the area and carved up riverbanks and shorelines.
Even so, in Mike's view people were far less reliable,
no matter how much nurturing they received. Linda was
testament to that. And for all of the dedicated nurturing
he gave to Jessie, the results were unpredictable, as well.

That didn't mean he would ever stop trying, but he needed one part of his life—his work—that he could count on and control to some degree.

Each day when he drove past Rose Cottage, he looked for evidence that Melanie D'Angelo had clipped back the first rosebush, but so far the garden was as much a disaster as ever. Despite his own best advice to stay the hell away, it grated on him that she'd done absolutely nothing. It was almost as if she were deliberately defying him. But that was absurd, of course. Why would a stranger's opinion matter to her one way or the other? She was clearly perfectly comfortable with the over-grown surroundings. Maybe she didn't intend to stick around long enough for any of it to matter.

When he pulled off the road in front of the house, he told himself it was only because he had an hour to kill before his next appointment. He told himself he was only being neighborly, reassuring himself that Melanie hadn't been overcome by dust, squeezed to death by a tenacious honeysuckle vine or attacked by a stray water moccasin.

When she didn't respond to his knock with that lethal lamp in her hand, he went looking for her. That it also gave him a chance to explore the rest of the property was purely a side benefit.

As he'd expected, the view was magnificent, with crabbing boats on the horizon and sunshine glittering on the gentle swells of the bay. Old oak trees and a line of weeping willows near the water's edge dappled the over-grown lawn with shade. There were more eyesores, though. A now-dead oak had been ripped from the ground by the hurricane, its roots exposed and as tall as a house. It had lain there so long it had destroyed everything beneath it. Other trees had been split, most likely by lightning, and should have been trimmed back long ago if there was to be any chance to save them.

At first, with so many downed trees and plants to draw his attention, he almost missed Melanie, but he finally spotted her at the back edge of the lawn, sitting on a weathered glider, her shoulders hunched, one foot tucked under her, the other pushing the swing idly to and fro. She looked so thoroughly dejected and defeated he almost turned and left her to her obvious misery, but he couldn't bring himself to do it. Six years after learning the hardest lesson of his life, and he was apparently still a sucker for a vulnerable woman.

"Melanie?" He spoke her name softly, but she jumped just the same, sending tea splashing out of her cup and onto her long, bare legs.

"Damn, I'm sorry," he apologized, offering her a handkerchief to wipe up the mess.

"Do you intend to make a habit of starting my day by scaring me half to death?" she inquired irritably.

"Apparently so," he said with a shrug. "Sorry. Want me to leave?"

She actually took her time answering, which told him she was seriously weighing her options.

"No, I suppose not. Now that you're here, you might as well sit down," she said grudgingly. She slid over to make room for him on the swing.

Mike hesitated. The swing wasn't all that wide. Sitting beside her would put her a little too close for comfort.

"If you don't sit, I'll have to stand," she said eventually. "Looking up at you is giving me a crick in my neck."

Since there was no alternative other than the overgrown lawn, Mike sat on the swing, keeping a careful distance between them. "You haven't done much work on the yard yet,'' he noted, figuring he'd be safer if he put her on the defensive.

''I don't even know where to begin. Besides, I'm still trying to deal with the house.''

He regarded her skeptically.

She immediately bristled. ''Hey, don't look at me like that. I *have* been working. In fact, once I got started, I decided the living room could use a fresh coat of paint and maybe some new curtains. That's made everything else look shabby, so the whole project has gotten out of hand. I've done nothing but paint for days now.''

He didn't even try to contain his surprise. ''You've painted the entire house since I last saw you?''

''Most of it,'' she said. ''I haven't gotten to the attic bedrooms yet.''

''When? How?''

She grinned. ''Don't tell me you're actually impressed with something I've done.''

Mike didn't want to concede that he was. ''Haven't seen the job yet, have I?''

''Oh, come on, admit it. You didn't think I was going to lift a finger to put things right around here, did you? You probably thought I'd turn a blind eye to the work that needed to be done or, worse, just give up and run away.''

''To be honest, that thought did occur to me. Why didn't you?''

''No place else I wanted to be,'' she admitted.

Her eyes were filled with that same sorrow he'd noted on his last visit. It made him want to hold her. To fight the urge, he balled his hands into fists and dug his nails into his palms.

''What's wrong with home?'' he asked.

"If you're referring to the place where my parents live, there's nothing wrong with it."

"You're still living with your folks?"

She gave him a wry look. "You're going to keep poking at this, aren't you?"

"Just being neighborly."

"Well, then, let me make it as plain as I possibly can. I don't want to talk about Boston or my past."

Mike could understand that kind of reluctance all too well. "Okay. Then that brings us back to this place."

She gave him a faint grin. "Actually, Mr. Mikelewski—"

"Mike."

"Mike, then. When it comes to this place, I think you'll find I'm full of surprises. Once I get around to these gardens, I intend to see that you're awed and amazed. By the time I leave—"

He gave her a sharp look. He'd expected as much, so he was surprised by the disappointment that slashed through him. "You're not here to stay?"

"Nope. Just passing through."

That made her willingness to do anything at all to bring the place back to its former beauty all the more remarkable. He should have felt a wave of relief at the news that she wasn't staying, but he didn't. He told himself it was because there was no way she could turn this garden around on some two-week vacation or whatever she was taking here.

"That makes it even more important that you consider my offer of help," he told her. "You won't be able to accomplish much on your own during a brief vacation."

She gave him a long, steady look, then nodded. "I'll keep that in mind. And for the record, I'm not exactly on vacation. It's more like a sabbatical."

"How long?"

"I'm not sure."

He saw her evasiveness as just more evidence that she couldn't be counted on to make a real difference here. "Say you do all this work," he said, regarding her curiously, "who'll look after it once you're gone? Or do you plan to abandon it again?"

"To be honest, I hadn't thought that far ahead," she told him. "Right now I'm barely planning this afternoon, much less tomorrow or next week."

"Drifting's fine for a time," he said. He'd done his share in those first weeks after he and Linda had separated. Only Jessie's demand for attention had kept him focused at all. He glanced at the woman next to him and added, "But making it a way of life is dangerous."

"Oh?" she asked, her tone edgy. "Do you have a lot of experience drifting along?"

Mike thought about the question before responding. When it came to emotional drifting, he'd become a grand champion, but having Jessie hadn't allowed him to drift in any other way for long. She forced him to live in the moment, since plans could get scrambled in a heartbeat on one of her bad days.

"Everyone needs goals," he said at last.

She regarded him curiously. "What are yours?"

The conversation was getting way too serious and increasingly personal. Mike grinned, taking that as his cue to leave before he did or said something he'd regret. "I only have one goal that concerns you…getting you to fix up this garden." He winked at her. "See you around."

On his way back to his car, Mike couldn't resist taking a peek in the front window. His jaw dropped. Melanie had indeed painted. The walls, which had been a dingy cream on his last visit, were now a sunny yellow. The trim was white, and the sheer curtains billowing at the windows were fresh as a breeze. A blue-and-white spatterware pitcher held a bouquet of daffodils. If every room had been transformed like this one, Melanie D'Angelo was going to bring Rose Cottage back to life.

He couldn't help wondering, though, what it was going to take to put a sparkle back into her eyes.

"Not my job," he told himself grimly, then wondered why the hell he'd needed to utter the obvious warning. It should have been a given.

Maybe it had something to do with the fact that the whole time he'd been sitting in that swing he'd wanted to haul her into his arms and kiss her until that sad mouth of hers curved into a smile. That was damn dangerous thinking for a man who'd vowed never to get involved in another relationship that could break either his heart or his daughter's.

Melanie was feeling inspired. The living room at Rose Cottage had turned out so well that she was ready to tackle the rest of the house. She'd gone through a dozen different decorating magazines and turned down the corners of every color scheme that appealed to her.

Now she was on a mission to see what she could find in the local stores to use as some sort of centerpiece— a piece of pottery, a painting, throw pillows—in each room to set the tone she wanted to achieve. Since she was unemployed and using her dwindling savings to accomplish the makeover, she had to be frugal. Fortunately, there were all sorts of antique shops tucked away in the Northern Neck, and not all of them dealt with high-end items she couldn't possibly afford. Besides, she liked the idea of bringing in things with a history.

For her own room she was looking for the shades of the sea—blue, soft green, pale gray—but she couldn't quite resist an occasional burst of orange or pink or even red in an old picture for the walls or a pillow that could be tossed on the bed. After all, even the tranquil bay turned brilliant shades of orange at sunset.

She'd just emerged from a shop in the neighboring town of Kilmarnock, feeling triumphant about finding a cobalt blue pitcher inside, when she spotted Mike's truck across the street. Her heart did a little stutter-step of anticipation. Because of that, she would have hurried on, but he came out of the real estate office and immediately spotted her.

Crossing the street with his long stride, he studied her with his usual solemn expression. "You look pleased with yourself," he concluded.

She lifted the bag containing her treasured pitcher. "Successful bargain hunting," she told him. Because she couldn't resist, she pulled the dark blue pitcher from the bag and held it up to the light, which made the old glass sparkle like sapphires. "Isn't it amazing?"

His gaze was on her, not the pitcher at all, when he echoed, "Amazing."

Her heart skipped a beat under that intense gaze. "You're not looking at the pitcher."

He shrugged and dutifully shifted his gaze. "It's a nice one, all right. It would look good with flowers in it."

She laughed. "Do you ever think about anything besides gardens?"

"Sure."

"Such as?"

"Have lunch with me and I'll tell you."

The faintly flirtatious words seemed to catch him by

surprise as much as they did her. Melanie was tempted to refuse, but the idea of another lonely meal back at the house held no appeal. Even the company of this dour man with the one-track mind was more intriguing than eating one more tuna on rye by herself.

"Sure," she said at last.

When they walked into the brightly lit café, it was already crowded with a mix of locals and tourists, each type readily identifiable. The locals wore slacks, long-sleeved shirts and ties or dresses and heels, while the tourists were armed with cameras, maps and local guide-books.

Mike spotted a table in the back and led the way, pausing to greet several people he knew. By the time they'd reached the vacant table, he'd introduced Melanie to so many friendly people, many of whom had known her grandmother, that the names were a jumble in her head.

A pretty blond waitress in her late twenties made a harried pass by their table to drop off menus and water. Melanie noticed that, rushed as she was, the woman managed a warm, lingering smile for Mike. He, however, barely seemed to notice.

"The crab cakes are good here," Mike told Melanie without bothering to pick up the menu himself. "And the burgers."

"How's the grilled-chicken caesar salad?" Melanie asked and got a raised eyebrow in response. She chuckled. "Too girlie for you?"

"Hey, I burn a lot of calories in my work. I need more protein than some little chicken breast and a bunch of lettuce leaves for lunch," he said disdainfully.

"And the fries that go with the burger, are they an important source of sustenance, too?"

"Absolutely," he said, poker-faced. "But it's the chocolate shake that really keeps me going."

To Melanie's surprise, after days of having very little appetite, her mouth was suddenly watering. "I'll have that, then."

"The shake?"

"No, all of it," she said decisively.

His eyes widened. "All of it?"

"Burger, fries and shake," she confirmed. "If the pies are homemade, I might have to have dessert, too."

When the waitress returned, she gave Melanie only a passing glance before focusing her attention on Mike.

"How've you been? I haven't seen you and Jess in here in ages."

Mike seemed vaguely uncomfortable. "We've been busy." He gestured in Melanie's direction. "Have you met Melanie D'Angelo? She's living at the Lindsey place. Cornelia Lindsey was her grandmother. Melanie, this is Brenda Chatham. She owns this place."

Brenda barely spared a nod in Melanie's direction— acknowledged and dismissed—before giving Mike another broad smile. "How about that dinner I've been promising you? I have an awesome recipe for barbecued ribs."

Mike frowned. "Thanks, anyway, but my schedule's pretty tight right now. Speaking of that, we'd better get our orders in so I can get back to work."

Brenda didn't even try to hide her disappointment. "Your usual?"

Mike nodded. "And Melanie will have the same. How do you want your burger, sweetheart?"

Melanie ignored the endearment, because she saw exactly what he was trying to do, create an intimacy between them that would finally get Brenda's attention. "Medium rare," she told Brenda.

"Sure thing," Brenda said.

After she'd gone, Mike regarded Melanie with a rueful expression. "Sorry about that. Brenda has some crazy idea that we'd make a good couple. I've tried to set her straight, but she's persistent."

"Have you considered just telling her you're not interested?"

He looked horrified at the thought. "Wouldn't that be rude?"

Melanie couldn't help chuckling, though she should have found his lack of candor troubling. "Actually I'd prefer to think of it as being honest, assuming you really aren't interested. She is an attractive woman, after all."

He stared in the direction of the kitchen, looking perplexed. "Is she?"

A man who didn't notice a willing blonde with huge brown eyes and a gorgeous figure? Melanie shook her head. She hadn't realized such men existed. Of course, maybe his lack of interest had something to do with the mysterious Jess Brenda had mentioned. "Who's Jess?"

Mike seemed taken aback by the question. "My daughter," he said eventually. "She's six. Most people call her Jessie."

Memories of Jeremy and his silence on the subject of his very real family slammed into her. "When were you planning on telling me about her?" she asked tightly.

His gaze narrowed. "It's not as if she's a secret. Most people in town know I have a child."

"I didn't."

"Okay, then, now you know. I have a daughter."

"And a wife?"

"No," he said tersely, almost as visibly tense now as Melanie was. "Let's talk about something else."

"Such as?"

"Boston and why you ran away from it," he suggested.

Melanie immediately saw what he was doing. She had her off-limits topics and so did he. She couldn't shake the feeling, though, that she at least needed to know if Jess's mother was completely out of the picture or not.

"One last question and I'll get off the subject of your personal life, okay?"

He gave her a grim look. "You can ask, but I reserve the right not to answer."

"Are you and Jess's mother divorced?"

"Yes."

Relief, out of all proportion given the circumstances, flooded through her. Whatever secrets Mike had about his family, at least she knew they weren't likely to come back and bite her in the butt the way Jeremy's had. Of course, the tension in his shoulders and the dark shadows in his eyes suggested there were things he *was* hiding.

So what? she chided herself. It wasn't as if she were dating the man. This was a casual lunch with a near stranger who'd offered to save her from another lonely meal. Nothing more. She was only here for a few weeks, anyway. Nothing would come of it, even if she were inclined to let another man into her life—which she wasn't.

The burgers arrived just then. Brenda plunked Melanie's down with a little less care than she did Mike's. It also looked suspiciously as if it had been deliberately burned to a crisp. Melanie put ketchup and mustard on it without comment.

"Trade with me," Mike said at once, his expression grim.

She stared at him. "Why? You didn't order yours burned, either."

"No, but yours came that way because of me. I'll eat it."

"Mike, it's okay. Really." She bit into the burger to prove the point, then chewed the tough-as-leather meat as if it were the best she'd ever eaten.

He sighed, then looked around till he caught Brenda's eye. "Brenda, there's a little problem here. Melanie's burger is beyond well done. She ordered medium rare. So, since we're both on a schedule, here's what we'll do. Her meal is going to be on the house, okay? And the next time I bring her in here, you're going to go out of your way to see that her food is prepared exactly the way she orders it."

Melanie wasn't sure whether her mouth or Brenda's dropped more, but they were both obviously startled by Mike's deadly serious tone.

"You think I did that on purpose?" Brenda demanded, using indignation rather effectively.

"I know you did."

"I'm not the cook," she reminded him.

"But you do write the tickets, and Boomer wouldn't do a thing on that grill except what you tell him to do," Mike said. "He knows you'll fire him otherwise."

Brenda forced a tight smile and turned to Melanie. "Sorry about the mix-up. The lunch is on me."

"That's not necessary," Melanie began, only to have Mike interrupt.

"Oh, yes, it is," he said. "Brenda wants all of her regular customers to go away happy, don't you?"

"I pride myself on it," Brenda said, not looking any too happy herself.

"Thank you, then," Melanie said graciously. "I know anyone can have an off day in the kitchen. I'm sure that's what happened here."

"Exactly," Brenda said, seizing on the proffered out. "Boomer's a little distracted today, that's all it is. I'd better go have a talk with him."

After she'd gone, Melanie frowned at Mike. "You didn't need to make such a big deal out of it, you know."

"Yes, I did. Weren't you the one who said Brenda deserved honesty?"

Melanie bit back a grin. "I was referring to your disinclination to go out with her."

He shrugged. "Honesty is honesty. I'll work up to the other thing."

"You're just afraid if you tell her, once and for all, that you're not interested, she'll start burning your burgers," Melanie accused.

"Damn straight," he agreed without the slightest sign of repentance.

"Can I ask you another personal question?" When he didn't immediately shake his head, she went on, "She's an attractive woman and she seems nice enough. Why aren't you interested?"

"My life's complicated enough. I'm not looking for a relationship."

Melanie could relate to that. "And I imagine it's a whole lot easier to give a rosebush what it needs than it is to deal with a woman."

His lips quirked slightly. "Couldn't have said it better myself."

Even though she could relate all too well to where he

was coming from, some traitorous little voice deep inside her couldn't help murmuring, "Lucky rosebush."

Mike regarded her oddly. "What was that?"

Oh, Lord, had she really said that out loud? "Nothing," she insisted, her cheeks burning.

"I thought you said something about the rosebushes," he persisted.

She feigned confusion. "Really? I was thinking about what you've been saying about what bad shape they're in. Maybe I said something about that without thinking."

A grin tugged at his lips. "Now who's being dishonest, darlin'?"

"I'm not your darling," she said irritably.

"I notice you didn't deny being dishonest, though. Maybe you're just telling a little white lie to spare my feelings."

She frowned at him. "Are you always this impossible?"

He laughed at that. "So they say." He stood up and grabbed the check. "Gotta run, darlin'."

She was about to utter yet another protest at the endearment when she spotted Brenda heading their way. To Melanie's shock, Mike leaned down and brushed a kiss across her lips. No doubt it was only meant to add to the impression that they were a couple, but Melanie's lips felt singed, anyway. She couldn't have uttered a word if her life depended on it. Instead, she grabbed her shake with trembling fingers and drank the last drops of thick chocolate. It was still deliciously cold, but it wasn't half as frosty as the look Brenda gave her when she finally managed to make her exit. She had a feeling that through no fault of her own, she'd just made her first enemy in town.

Chapter Three

It was the scent of lilacs that brought Melanie out of the house on a rainy Saturday morning the second week in April. It had been years since she'd smelled that aroma, and it never failed to remind her of her grandmother. For all the showy roses in her grandmother's garden, it was the lilacs she'd loved most. She'd filled the house with huge vases of them during the short blooming season. And, rain or shine, she'd thrown open the windows for yet more of their sweet scent.

Now, though, the clusters of lavender flowers were fighting for breath on the overgrown bushes that had been invaded by the twisting vines of honeysuckle. Melanie stared at the mess with dismay, understanding fully for the first time why Mike was so thoroughly disgusted by the neglect. These once-thriving bushes were about to be destroyed.

Inspired to save the lilacs, she went inside, found the

key to the garden shed, then headed outdoors with some trepidation to see what tools were available. With any luck, she wouldn't find any snakeskins dangling on the hooks along with the clippers and rakes.

It took several tries to get the old key to work in the rusty lock on the shed, but inside she found every gardening tool imaginable, all kept in pristine condition aside from way too many spiderwebs to suit her. She gingerly selected one and wiped it off with the old rag she'd brought with her, then went outside to begin the daunting task of putting things to rights in the garden.

Oblivious to the light rain, she began snipping the honeysuckle vines, then tugging the endless strands out of the bushes and piling them into a garbage can. Yanking the roots from the ground was an even more thankless task, one that quickly had her sweating and cursing a blue streak.

She'd filled three cans when she heard the crunch of tires on gravel and a car engine cut off out front. A door slammed, then there was a low murmur of voices suddenly punctuated by a scream.

"No, Daddy! No!"

Melanie dropped her clippers and ran to the front to find Mike bent over beside the car trying to extricate a screaming, kicking child.

"What on earth?" she murmured.

Mike's head snapped up and hit the edge of the door frame.

"Don't get any wild ideas," he said, looking thoroughly defeated. "My daughter's terrified of this place for some reason. She thinks it's haunted."

Melanie took in his weary expression, then glanced at the stricken child whose sobs were finally beginning to lessen as she eyed Melanie with wariness. Nudging Mike aside, Melanie said, "Let me give it a try, okay? I assume this is Jessie."

"Right."

Melanie gazed into deep-blue eyes, several shades darker than her father's. They were glistening with tears. Her fine blond hair was slipping free of a bright-pink scrunchie.

"Hey, Jessie. I'm Melanie," she said quietly. "I live here."

The little girl stared back solemnly, taking in that news. Melanie waited.

"Are you a ghost?" Jessie finally asked in a voice barely above a frightened whisper.

Melanie bit back a smile. "I don't think so. Want to find out for sure?"

Jessie looked intrigued. "How?"

"Pinch me."

"Really?" Jessie glanced up at her father, who shrugged.

"Won't it hurt?" she asked Melanie, her brow creased in a worried frown.

"Not if I'm a ghost."

Jessie reached out with her dainty little hand and gently pinched Melanie's arm.

"Ouch," Melanie said with an exaggerated grimace.

"I'm sorry," Jessie whispered at once.

"It's okay. I guess we know now that I'm not a ghost, right?"

"I guess so," Jessie said, though she still sounded doubtful.

"Want to come into the house?" Melanie asked. "We can check to see if there are any ghosts inside, and your dad can chase them away. What do you think?"

Jessie nodded shyly and held out her arms. Melanie

released the seat belt, then lifted the girl out and set her on the ground. She immediately clutched Melanie's hand.

When they stepped through the gate, Melanie caught the look of surprise in Mike's eyes when he spotted the cans filled with vines.

"Been working, I see," he said.

"For hours."

"It's a start," he said grudgingly.

Melanie stared at him. "That's all you have to say?"

A smile tugged at the corners of his mouth. "That's all you've done."

Because Jessie was regarding them with another worried frown, Melanie held back the sharp retort she wanted to make. Instead, she asked, "Why are you here, Mike? Did you stop by just to annoy me?"

"Actually we came because we're going to a nursery over in White Stone. I thought you might want to ride along and get some ideas."

Melanie gave him a wry look. "Don't you think I should get rid of what I have before I start thinking about what to put in the ground?"

"Never hurts to plan ahead. Bring that picture you showed me. I'll show Jessie the swing while you get it."

His arrogant assumption that she would fall in with his plans was almost enough to force a rebellion, but something about Mike Mikelewski's quiet determination to restore her grandmother's gardens got to her. Since he hadn't asked for a dime for his advice or his help, she had to assume it was because he genuinely cared about setting the neglected landscape to rights. She'd be foolish to ignore such an offer out of pure stubbornness.

Even so, a cautionary alarm sounded in her head. Mike might be divorced, but his tense tone the other day suggested there was not only an ex-wife lurking some-where, but quite possibly an ex-wife who liked to stir up trouble. Melanie wasn't inclined to get tangled up in the middle of that kind of complicated situation.

She'd make this innocuous enough trip to the nursery with Mike because it was something she'd need to do sooner or later, anyway. But after this, she vowed, she'd discourage any further contact between them.

Not that Mike had actually shown one iota of personal interest in her, she was forced to admit. But every time she looked into his eyes, she suddenly wanted things she'd sworn never to allow into her life again. And that wouldn't do. It wouldn't do at all.

"I promised Jessie a tour of the house," she told him. "We're ghost busting."

His lips quirked at that. "Then, by all means, let's go inside."

"You're in charge of banishing any ghosts we find," Melanie added.

He nodded. "Got it."

Jessie peered up at him. "Are you scared, Daddy?"

"Nah," he said. "No silly old ghost is a match for me."

While Mike was showing Jessie around and conduct-ing dramatic searches of closets and cupboards for signs of ghosts, Melanie took the time to wash her hands and run a brush through her tangled hair.

"No ghosts," Mike eventually hollered from down-stairs. "We're going out to the swing."

"I'll be right there," Melanie called back.

On her way out, she grabbed the photo of the garden. Outside, she could hear Jessie's squeals of delight echo-ing from the backyard. Obviously, her earlier fears had been calmed by her father's ghost-busting expedition.

Melanie rounded the house and spotted the little girl sitting atop Mike's broad shoulders as he stood at the water's edge. She had her hands fisted in his hair in a way that had to hurt like the dickens, but he wasn't complaining.

"Daddy, no!" Jessie shouted, giggling.

"You don't want to go for a swim?" he teased, taking another step toward the bay.

"No!"

Melanie listened to them for several minutes, enjoying the banter and feeling just a little like an outsider. Oddly, it reminded her of the way she'd felt when Jeremy had finally admitted the truth about his family. Aside from the burst of anger, she'd immediately known he had something important that was missing from her life, something she might never have. It was as if she were being taunted by possibilities, and the unfairness of it had hurt.

Mike chose that moment to turn around, and the laughter on his lips promptly died. He studied her intently. "Everything okay?"

Melanie forced a smile. "Fine."

"You saved me," Jessie told her. "Daddy was going to make me swim in the water and it's too cold."

"Oh, I don't think you were ever at risk," Melanie told her. "Something tells me your dad takes very good care of you."

Jessie nodded. "He does, but he's not a mom. Moms know it's too soon to go swimming."

Melanie didn't miss the tiny flash of hurt in Mike's eyes, but he didn't respond.

"Dads know stuff like that, too," Melanie assured Jessie. "My dad used to take my sisters and me to Cape Cod in the summer, and he knew all the important stuff about swimming. My mom never even got her toes wet.''

Jessie studied her solemnly, as if she were trying to process such a thing. ''Not even once?''

''Never,'' Melanie told her. ''So, you see, it seems to me like you haven't been giving your dad nearly enough credit.''

Mike gave her a grateful look as he tucked Jessie into the back seat and snapped the seat belt.

''My dad knows lots about flowers and stuff,'' Jessie volunteered proudly, obviously eager to jump on the bandwagon about her father's unique talents. ''People pay him to make their gardens grow. He's teaching me.''

''And do you have your own garden?'' Melanie asked her.

Jessie nodded. ''I will this summer. It's gonna have squashes and tomatoes and beans for the bunnies.''

Melanie chuckled. ''I thought people ate beans.''

''They do, but bunnies like them better than I do, so I'm growing them just for the bunnies. I got it all planned out. We're gonna buy seeds today. I get to pick 'em out.'' She peered intently at Melanie. ''What are you gonna plant in your garden?''

''I'm not sure,'' Melanie admitted. ''Your dad's going to help me figure that out.''

''You probably need to grow some beans, too,'' Jessie advised her. ''There's lots and lots of bunnies and I can't feed 'em all.''

Melanie chuckled. ''I'll think about that.''

''I think we're going to concentrate on flowers for Melanie's garden today,'' Mike chimed in. He glanced at her. ''And maybe think about an herb garden.''

Melanie envisioned how happy an herb garden would

make Maggie. "Definitely," she said. "Though I don't recall my grandmother having one."

"You don't have to recreate what she had exactly," Mike said. "Gardens evolve over time. Personally, I like a combination of the beautiful and the practical, but not everybody cares about growing their own food or herbs, not when there are farmer's markets all over this area offering fresh produce."

"I wouldn't mind growing tomatoes," Melanie said, thinking of how fabulous it would be to pick one for dinner and slice it to serve with mozzarella cheese and fresh basil, also from her own garden. Never mind that she was unlikely to be here when the time came to harvest the tomatoes.

Mike gave her a lingering look. "There you go," he teased. "You're beginning to envision the possibilities."

"How long does it take for a tomato plant to produce its first ripe tomato?" she asked.

"Sixty days or so, depending on the variety and the weather," he replied.

"Too long," she said, unable to contain a sigh of regret.

"Maybe you'll decide to stick around."

She shook her head. "Impossible."

"You have a job to get back to?"

"No."

"A boyfriend?"

"No."

"Then what's to stop you from staying till you pick your first homegrown tomato?"

"I don't have an endless supply of money," she told him frankly. "Sooner or later I'll have to go back to Boston and find another job."

"Find one here," he said. "There's lots of seasonal

work, if you don't want something permanent. Hell, Brenda's always complaining that she can't find good summer help for the restaurant.''

Melanie laughed. "Yes, I imagine she'd be absolutely delighted to hire me, since we got off to such a great start.''

"I could put in a word for you," he offered.

"Thanks, but if I should happen to decide to stick around, I'm capable of finding my own job. And having you intercede for me with Brenda would only add fuel to the resentment she already feels toward me.''

"You have a point," he agreed. "What field were you in before?''

"My degree's in marketing, but I took a job as a receptionist when I got out of college.''

He shot her a disbelieving look. "How long ago was that?''

"Not that long ago," she said defensively. "I worked my way through college—waiting tables, as a matter of fact—so I've only been out a couple of years.''

"You have a degree in marketing, but you've been working as a receptionist? Are entry-level jobs in marketing that tough to find?''

"Actually this one was supposed to lead to a promotion, but it didn't work out that way," she said, unable to keep a defensive note out of her voice. She could hear how ridiculous it sounded that she'd wasted so much time waiting for the right chance to come along, instead of making it happen.

The management at Rockingham Industries had dangled the prospect of a marketing position in front of her, but she realized now that she'd made herself all but indispensable as a receptionist, doing the job so well that they'd left her right where she was. Jeremy had repeatedly promised to remind the executives that she was a good candidate to move up into his department, but somehow it had never happened. What a fool she'd been!

Fortunately Mike pulled into a parking lot at the nursery just then, so she didn't have to try to defend her decision. She scrambled out of the car and would have gone on ahead, if Jessie hadn't demanded that Melanie be the one to take her out of the car.

Mike gave Melanie an apologetic look. "Would you mind? Once she gets an idea into her head, there's no peace unless I go along with it. Some things aren't worth arguing over."

"No problem," Melanie assured him, helping Jessie out of the car. When the girl tucked her hand trustingly into Melanie's, something in Melanie's heart flipped over.

"Can you help me pick out seeds?" Jessie asked. "I know where they are."

"Wouldn't you rather have your dad do that? He's the expert."

"I want you to do it," Jessie insisted. *"Please!"*

There was an unmistakable edge of hysteria in the little girl's voice that caught Melanie by surprise. She glanced toward Mike.

"It's okay," he said. "If you don't mind taking her, it might be easier. I'll fill you in later."

Melanie nodded. She smiled down at Jessie. "Okay, then. It looks as if you and I are on a mission, Jessie. Show me those seeds."

When Jessie tugged her off in the direction of the seeds, Melanie glanced back and caught Mike's expression. He looked almost as bewildered and dismayed as she felt.

"Over here," Jessie said, giving Melanie's hand another tug. "See? Look at all the pretty pictures." She headed straight for a selection of vegetable seeds. She studied them as intently as another child might contemplate a video choice, then gave a little sigh.

"Is something wrong?" Melanie asked.

"I like these," Jessie admitted, "'cause you can see what they'll look like."

"Is there a problem with that?"

"Daddy says the best ones are over there, in those bins," Jessie explained. "There aren't any pictures, so how can you tell if you'll like them?"

"Experience," Melanie said. "I imagine farmers know which ones produce the best crops, so they don't need to see a picture every time." Melanie took her over to the bins of seeds. "See, right here it says these seeds are for Silver Queen corn. I've had that, and it's the sweetest and best ever. I don't need to see a picture to know it's good."

Jessie regarded her with wide eyes. "We could grow corn?"

Melanie laughed at her amazement. "If you have enough room in your garden, you can."

"Daddy never said that, and we've got lots and lots of room. I want some of those seeds," she said at once.

Melanie filled a small bag for her, then labeled it. "Now what?"

"Read me another sign," Jessie commanded. "One for beans."

Melanie found several bins of bean seeds and read the labels.

Jessie peered at them worriedly. "Which ones do you think the bunnies will like best?"

"I imagine they'll be happy with whichever ones you choose," she said honestly. "But I'd pick these."

"Okay," Jessie said readily, reaching for the scoop and a bag that was way too big.

"Whoa!" Melanie protested. "Not so many. You just need a few."

"But I told you, we got lots and lots of bunnies."

"Even so, a few seeds will give you more than enough beans." She handed the child a small bag. "Fill this one up. Then let's go and find your dad."

When they found Mike, he was pushing a cart overflowing with small plants and shrubs. Melanie eyed it warily. "You've gone a little overboard, haven't you? We never talked about planting bushes."

He laughed. "I do have other jobs," he told her. "Some people actually hire me to do this."

"Of course," she said at once, chagrined. "Is any of that for me?"

"I picked out some perennials for you. I went by what I saw in the picture. These are hollyhocks," he said, showing her a half-dozen plants. "And summer phlox." He gestured toward a larger plant. "Foxglove. And back here are some daylilies we can plant in clusters. It's not much, but it's a start. I didn't want to get too much until we've cleaned out more of the weeds and gotten some decent topsoil in there." He met her gaze. "What do you think?"

"That I'm completely out of my element."

"Which is why I'll be around," he said. "That is, if you want my help."

She gave him a wry look. "I think we can both agree that it's going to be a necessity. We'll have to discuss your fees, though."

"No charge," he said at once.

"Mike, that's not right. You're a professional. I have to pay you."

He returned her look with a stubborn gaze. "Let's just say you've earned at least one afternoon of my time."

She gave him a perplexed look. "How?"

He nodded toward Jessie, who was sitting on the edge of the large cart contentedly counting out the bean seeds. "Keeping her occupied was a huge help to me."

"But all I did was help her pick out some seeds," Melanie protested.

"Which you apparently managed to do without her having a tantrum," Mike said. "I've never once accomplished that. In case you haven't noticed, Jessie can be headstrong."

"Most kids can be," Melanie said. "It just takes a little finesse to work around that."

"Finesse and patience," Mike corrected. "Sometimes I'm woefully lacking in both. Let's just say I'm grateful and leave it at that, okay?"

Melanie studied him and thought she detected sincere appreciation in his eyes. She wasn't entirely sure she understood it, but it was clear he thought he owed her.

"Thank you," she said at last. "I know wherever she is, my grandmother thanks you, too."

He chuckled. "And Lord knows I can use an angel looking out for me. Now let's pay for this stuff and get out of here while peace reigns."

"How about I treat us all to ice cream on the way home?" Melanie offered.

Jessie's head shot up. "Chocolate?"

"If that's what you want," Melanie agreed. "And if your dad says it's okay."

Mike grinned. "You'll never hear me saying no to ice cream, especially not chocolate, right, Jess?"

"That's 'cause it's the bestest," Jessie said solemnly.

"I agree," Melanie said. She leaned down. "You know how it's best of all?"

"How?"

"With hot fudge on top," Melanie said.

Mike groaned, even as Jessie's eyes lit up.

"Sundaes!" Jessie shouted.

"*You* are cleaning up the mess," Mike warned Melanie, his expression dire.

"No problem," Melanie said cheerfully.

He gave her a long, hard look, then chuckled. "That's what you think."

Chapter Four

Mike couldn't get over the fact that Jessie seemed to have taken such an instant liking to Melanie. She'd been on her best behavior for most of the day. He knew from bitter experience, though, that her good mood could end in a heartbeat. Even as he parked in front of the ice cream shop, he had this gut-deep sense of dread that they were testing his daughter's limits.

Still, once Melanie had mentioned ice cream, there had been no way to bow out of the excursion gracefully. That would have caused a scene, no question about it.

On the entire trip back to town from the nursery, Jessie had debated whether she wanted whipped cream and a cherry on top of her sundae. To her credit Melanie had shown endless patience with the drawn-out discussion. In fact, she'd seemed equally eager to decide on the merits of the extra toppings. Most people would have jumped screaming from the car after the first ten minutes. Hell, Mike was about ready to leap from the moving vehicle himself.

"Have you two decided yet?" he asked hopefully as they went inside. Thankfully the weather was cool enough that not too many people were interested in ice cream to beat the heat. The three of them had the place almost to themselves. He'd been here far too many times when the line had been long and Jessie hadn't been able to make up her mind which flavor she wanted. The decision-making process had taxed his patience, as well as that of most of the people in line behind them.

"I'm having chocolate ice cream and lots and lots of whipped cream on my hot-fudge sundae," Melanie said at once. "How about you, Jessie?"

"Me, too," The six-year-old responded eagerly, looking to Melanie for approval.

"Good choice," Melanie praised. "How about you, Mike?"

Stunned by the success of her clever tactic, he said, "Let's make it easy and make it three. You two find a table and I'll get the ice cream."

"No way," Melanie said. "This was my idea and my treat."

Jessie peered up at her. "But boys always pay when they take girls on a date, right, Daddy?"

"This isn't a date," Melanie said a little too firmly.

Her quick response made Mike all the more determined to act as if it were. "Close enough," he insisted, then gazed into her eyes. "Unless you want to arm wrestle me for the honors." He deliberately flexed his muscle, barely containing a grin as her eyes locked on his arm.

"Show-off," Melanie muttered, tearing her gaze away with unmistakable reluctance. "I won't create a scene and humiliate you by taking you on.'' She lifted her gaze to his. ''But we will debate this later.''

He nodded. He had a hunch he'd pushed the limits of her independent streak today. There was a spark of fire in her eyes that he'd never noticed before. He figured that had to be a good thing, given her apparent despondency and lack of interest when they'd first met, but it was probably something he didn't want to stir up too often.

Melanie led Jessie to a table and got her seated with an ease that once again surprised him. Maybe what Jessie had needed all along was a mother's touch. Maybe he was the one at fault all this time, the cause of her tantrums. Lord knew he'd made a lot of blunders while he'd been getting a grip on being a single dad.

But even as the thought occurred to him, Mike knew he was being foolish. Melanie was merely a novelty. She was giving Jessie the kind of undivided attention the child craved. His daughter's good behavior had nothing to do with Melanie's parenting skills versus his own, he reassured himself.

But as reasonable as that explanation was, he still found it irritating that Melanie seemed to have some sort of knack for calming his daughter. Realizing he was actually jealous of the woman, instead of being grateful and admiring, he bit back a curse at his own stupidity.

When he arrived at the table with the ice cream, Jessie was chattering like a little magpie about school and her friends. Mike learned more in five minutes than he had on a dozen rides home. Once again that nasty little trace of resentment crept over him, but he forced it back down and concentrated instead on his sundae.

''I dropped it!''

Out of the blue, Jessie's voice rose to a wail, drawing the attention of everyone in the shop.

"It's okay," Melanie murmured, wiping up the spoonful of ice cream that had fallen into Jessie's lap before Mike could react.

"No, it's all ruined," Jessie insisted, throwing her spoon across the room. "I hate ice cream."

She was about to knock her bowl from the table, when Mike snatched it out of reach.

"That's enough," he said firmly.

"But it's mine," Jessie screamed, trying to hit him.

For just an instant, Melanie looked stunned by the unexpected burst of temper. Mike waited for her to announce a sudden need for a trip to the bathroom or some other escape, but instead, she calmly pushed her own bowl of ice cream away.

"I've had enough, too," she said as if more than half of her sundae weren't still in the bowl. "Jessie, why don't you and I go outside and wait for your dad?"

Mike started to protest, but she gave a slight shake of her head.

"Come on, Jessie. I think I saw some really cool books in the store next door. Want to go look at them?"

Jessie sniffed and blinked back tears, clearly torn between escalating her tantrum and the offer of a trip to the bookstore. She looked at Mike as if he might say something that would tilt the decision one way or another. Instead, taking his cue from Melanie, he simply waited silently for Jessie to make up her mind.

Eventually she scrambled out of her chair and tucked her hand in Melanie's. "Can I get a book about crabs?" she asked hopefully.

"If they have one," Melanie promised.

Jessie beamed. "They do. It's a whole series. I have two, but there are more."

"Then we'll find one," Melanie said.

And then they were gone. Mike stared after them, not sure whether to sigh or laugh. He couldn't very well allow Melanie to bribe his daughter every time she threatened to throw a tantrum, but he had to admit that it had worked like a charm just now.

Or maybe it wasn't the promise of a bribe at all, but simply the distraction. Melanie had taken Jessie's attention off of her frustration and focused it on something else. Maybe there was a lesson for him in that, if he wasn't too busy feeling jealous to learn it.

He contemplated that as he slowly ate the rest of his sundae, barely tasting it but enjoying the brief reprieve. How had a single woman gained so much insight into his daughter in such a short time, when he spent most of his life being totally at a loss?

It was the novelty of it, he concluded once more. It had to be. Melanie could have endless patience because this was the first time she'd had to deal with Jessie's whims. His own patience was threadbare. Maybe he and his daughter needed to take more breaks from each other, but he'd avoided leaving her with sitters, mostly out of guilt. Without a mother in her life, Jessie needed his constant attention—or so he'd convinced himself. Could it be that he'd been wrong about that? Had she needed to be exposed to more people and more social situations than he'd permitted?

Whatever it was that gave Melanie such endless patience, he was grateful. Too bad she wasn't sticking around. Summer was just around the corner, and he was in desperate need of day care. He'd hire Melanie in a heartbeat, if she were willing. Jessie had pretty much worn out her welcome at every child-care center in the region, and taking her with him on jobs had proved to be frustrating for both of them.

The temptation to broach the subject anyway was almost too great to resist. What stopped him was the realization that it wasn't all about Jessie. He'd been more at peace today than he had been in a long time. There was something soothing about Melanie's company that worked its magic on him as well as his daughter.

And sharing the responsibility of caring for Jessie, even for a few hours, had shown him what life might have been like if things had turned out differently with Linda. He'd gotten a taste of being a real family, and the pitiful truth was, he'd liked it.

Was it possible that he'd been waiting all these years for someone like Melanie to come along? Someone who'd take them both on?

No, he said staunchly. Absolutely not!

But even as he mentally uttered the disclaimers, he could hear that they weren't ringing the least bit true. On some level, something had shifted today. Seeing Melanie had stopped being all about fixing up the Rose Cottage garden and had somehow gotten to be about healing his and Jessie's wounded hearts.

Jessie was a complicated and troubled little girl. Melanie had picked up on that even before Mike had hinted at it. The tantrum at the end of a long day wasn't that unusual, but there'd been plenty of other signs, including the way Mike tiptoed around his daughter as if he'd do just about anything to avoid an outburst. Naturally Jessie, being a smart kid, had caught on to that, and she knew just how to play him and his single-dad guilt.

Despite all the problems, Melanie couldn't help being

charmed by the six-year-old. She hadn't been around many children, but she'd discovered today that she loved the way Jessie's mind worked, the way her imagination knew no bounds. It was also a boon to her wounded pride to have the little girl regard her with undisguised adoration.

Of course, Melanie warned herself, it wasn't healthy to get too attached or to allow Jessie to become too attached to her. This was a one-time outing, not the start of something.

Still, she couldn't help liking the way Jessie snuggled against her as they sat on the floor in the children's section of the bookstore and pored over the selections.

"I like this one best," Jessie said, after they'd looked at a dozen or more choices. "Are you sure I can have it?"

"Absolutely. It's a present," Melanie said.

Jessie studied her worriedly. "You and my daddy are friends, right?"

"Yes," Melanie said, not sure why that was relevant.

"Then it's okay," Jessie concluded happily. "I couldn't take it if you were a stranger."

Ah! "No, you couldn't," Melanie agreed. "But we can check with your dad, if that would make you feel better."

Jessie eyed the book with longing. "He might say no," she said hesitantly.

"Leave your father to me," Melanie told her with a confidence she had no right to feel. She'd taken a lot for granted today. The mere fact that she'd insisted on bringing Jessie to the bookstore to avert a tantrum was probably more interference than some would have tolerated. But after an initial show of reluctance, Mike had actually looked relieved. She had a hunch he'd been at his wit's end with Jessie for some time now.

Suddenly Jessie jumped up and bolted, clutching the book. "Daddy, look at the present Melanie's getting me!"

Melanie gazed up into Mike's turbulent eyes and guessed that she'd overstepped. "It's just a book. And she read me the first page all by herself, so I thought she deserved it."

His gaze faltered at that. He hunkered down in front of Jessie. "You read the whole first page?"

"Uh-huh. Want to hear?"

"Absolutely."

She plopped right down on the floor in the middle of the aisle and opened the book on her lap. "Chadwick," she began, then looked at her father. "Remember him, Daddy? He's the crab."

Mike grinned, pride shining in his eyes. "I remember."

Jessie went on to read an entire sentence, slowly but without a single mistake. She gazed up at Mike. "Is that right?"

His smile spread. "Absolutely perfect. I guess the book is yours, but I'm buying it." He pulled some money from his pocket and gave it to her. "You take it up front where I can see you and pay for it."

"Okay," Jessie said happily and ran off.

"I would have bought it," Melanie told him. "I'm the one who made the deal with her."

"I know, but it's better this way."

"Why?"

"Because I don't want her to start to count on you."

"It's a book, Mike, not a commitment."

He regarded her with troubled eyes. "Not to Jessie.

Don't make promises to her, Melanie. Not when you're leaving.''

Suddenly she understood. "You're comparing me to her mother."

His expression turned dark. "You're nothing like Linda," he said bitterly. "But you will leave. You've told me that yourself. I have to protect her from that kind of disappointment. Kids tend to think abandonment is all about them, no matter how often you tell them otherwise.''

He walked away before she could think of anything to say. Besides, it wasn't the time or the place to pursue the subject, so Melanie simply followed him as he went after Jessie.

They drove back to her house in silence. Jessie had fallen asleep in the back seat, so Mike left her there and unloaded the plants quickly.

"Keep 'em watered till we can get them into the ground," he said when everything was out of the back of the truck. "I'll be by to help when I have some time."

"Sure," she said. "Thanks for taking me along today.''

He gave her a curt nod, then strode back to the car and drove off, leaving Melanie to stare after him and wonder about the woman who'd hurt him so badly he didn't trust Melanie not to do the same. Worse, she wasn't sure she wouldn't. The only way to be sure was to avoid getting involved with him and Jessie in the first place.

Melanie wasn't all that surprised when Mike showed up on her doorstep on Monday morning, most likely right after dropping Jessie off at school.

"Do you have a minute?" he asked, looking vaguely uneasy.

"Sure. Come on in. I just made coffee. Want some?"

"Coffee sounds great."

He took a seat at the kitchen table, but when Melanie had handed him his mug of coffee and seated herself across from him, he avoided her gaze. She could have let the silence go on, but it was beginning to get on her nerves.

"I suppose you came by to warn me again about getting too close to Jessie," she said. "I've thought about it, and I can see your point."

"Actually I came to apologize," he said, meeting her gaze. "I made it seem as if you'd done something wrong, when you'd been nothing but kind to her all day long. Most people wouldn't have jumped in to take charge when she was about to throw a tantrum. They'd have run for the hills."

"It wasn't a big deal. She's a great kid."

"She's a troubled kid," he corrected. "I'm sure you figured that out."

"Because you and her mom are divorced," Melanie said.

"That and..." He seemed to be struggling to find the right words. "Well, because her mom was addicted to drugs when Jessie was born. It's affected Jessie. She was born addicted, too."

"Oh, Mike, I'm so sorry."

"She's okay for the most part, but there are lingering effects, like the tantrums over nothing. One minute she's fine, the next she's out of control. It's like living with a time bomb, only I don't have any idea when it's set to go off."

Melanie's heart ached for both of them. "That must be incredibly frustrating for both of you."

He frowned. "I didn't come here so you could pity me. I just thought you should know why I'm so protective of her. Keeping Jessie on an even emotional keel is hard enough without people coming and going in her life."

Melanie wanted to argue that children needed to learn that people would always come and go, but how could she? Not only was it not her place, but it was probably entirely different for a child who'd lost her mother. Having that relationship severed at such an early age had to be traumatic. Additional losses would only bolster Jessie's fear that it was unsafe to give her love to anyone. It could have a lasting effect on her emotional well-being.

Before Melanie could think of what she could say, Mike stood up. "Well, that's all I wanted you to know. I'd better get going. I have a delivery at one of my jobs this morning, and I need to be there to supervise getting all the plants into the ground. I should be able to get by here to help you by midweek."

"Whenever it's convenient," she told him. "I just appreciate your willingness to take this on."

Melanie walked him back to the door. Impulsively, she reached up and touched his cheek. "You're a terrific dad, especially given the trying circumstances. I hope you know that."

Surprise flickered in his eyes. "What makes you say that?"

"You remind me of my own dad and, believe me, there's not a better one on earth. You're protective and attentive and you listen to Jessie. Most of all, it's obvious you adore her. She may miss having a mom in her life, but she's very lucky to have you.''

For an instant this hulking, strong man looked flustered. "I don't know what to say."

Melanie grinned at him. "It's a compliment. All you need to say is thank you."

Instead, to her astonishment, he leaned down and kissed her—just the slightest grazing of warm lips against hers, but it was enough to send heat spiraling through her.

Then he was out the door. He was halfway to the street when he finally glanced back and caught her with her fingers against her lips. He winked.

"Thanks," he said.

Now she was the one who was flustered. "Anytime," she whispered, but only when he was too far away to hear her.

This visit to Rose Cottage was supposed to provide her with a whole new level of serenity, but suddenly Melanie was feeling anything but serene. She'd felt more clear-to-her-toes shock waves from that innocent little kiss than she'd ever felt in Jeremy's arms. Now wasn't that interesting?

And dangerous.

Mike had worked like a demon all day, pushing himself in the vain hope that sweat and hard work would make him forget all about that kiss. It had happened on impulse, just a quick little brush of his mouth over hers, mostly to see if it would rattle her half as much as her kind words and solemn expression had rattled him.

The joke had turned out to be on him. His blood had been humming all day long, and the scent of her had lingered with him. Apparently there wasn't enough perspiration on the planet to overpower it.

"Hey, Mike, we're supposed to provide the labor," Jeff Clayborne shouted.

"I'm just helping out a little," Mike responded, pausing long enough to wipe his brow with the already-soaked bandanna he'd stuck in his back pocket.

"You help out any more and we'll be out of jobs," Jeff retorted. "Take a break, man. I've got a Thermos of iced tea here that I'll share with you."

Mike knew all about Jeff's tea. It was so sweet it was enough to send most people into a diabetic coma. Jeff said the key to getting it that way was to boil the sugar right into it. Mike shuddered at the thought.

"I'll pass on the tea, thanks, but I will take a break. I've got bottled water in my truck." He grabbed a bottle from the cooler in back, then joined the other man in the shade of an oak tree.

Jeff glanced over at him. "Something on your mind?"

"No. Why?"

"You usually work this hard when there's a problem with Jessie. Otherwise, you loaf around and supervise the rest of us."

"Very funny," Mike commented. "And you're totally off the mark. Jessie's great, actually."

"I imagine that has something to do with her new friend," Jeff said, his expression innocent.

Mike saw where this was going and wondered how word had gotten around so quickly. Then, again, this was a small town.

"What new friend would that be?" he asked, keeping his own expression neutral.

"I heard blond hair and big blue eyes and legs that

wouldn't quit.'' Jeff grinned wickedly. ''Oh, wait, she would be *your* new friend, right?''

''Go to hell,'' Mike muttered.

''Heard she's new in town, that she's Cornelia Lindsey's granddaughter and that the three of you were over at the nursery on Saturday, then at the ice cream shop and then the bookstore.''

''It's a damn good thing we weren't trying to sneak around,'' Mike muttered irritably.

Jeff laughed. ''Yeah, well, you definitely picked the wrong place to live if you ever hope to keep your personal life a secret. Besides, an awful lot of people have been trying to set you up ever since you moved here, including my wife. You've turned 'em all down. Naturally they're curious when you managed to find someone all on your own. The staff at the nursery couldn't wait to report to Pam and me.''

''Melanie doesn't have anything to do with my personal life,'' Mike insisted, figuring he would eventually burn in hell for the lie. ''She's a client. Sort of.''

''How does someone get to be a 'sort-of' client?'' Jeff taunted. ''Especially since you told me last week you weren't taking on any new jobs for a while.''

''I'm helping her get the garden fixed up at her grandmother's place.''

Jeff regarded him with amusement. ''And I imagine she's 'sort of' paying you for your help. Am I right? What's the going rate for that kind of help? Dinner? A roll in the hay?''

Mike scowled at him. ''It's not like that, dammit.''

Jeff held up his hands. ''Hey, okay. Don't get all worked up. I was just teasing.''

''Yeah. That's the kind of teasing that can ruin someone's reputation. Knock it off.''

Jeff's gaze narrowed. "Do you really have a thing for this woman?"

"No, absolutely not!" Mike responded fiercely.

Jeff studied him intently, then burst out laughing. "Oh, pal, you are in one helluva state of denial."

Mike glared at him. It was probably true, but his friend didn't need to be quite so gleeful about it. Mike stood up slowly, deliberately took his time over the last swallow of cool water from the bottle, then tossed it in a nearby trash bin. Only then did he meet Jeff's gaze.

"You don't know what you're talking about," he said quietly.

Jeff laughed. "Sure, I do. I said exactly the same thing about Pam till about fifteen minutes before the wedding ceremony. Denial's second nature to us, pal. Women know it, too. They just ignore our protests, and the next thing you know, *bam,* wedded bliss."

"Not gonna happen," Mike insisted. He'd been there, done that and lived to rue the day. Except for Jessie, he reminded himself quickly. She was worth all the rest.

She was also the reason why he'd never let things with Melanie go anywhere. Period.

He didn't waste his breath saying any of that to Jeff. Why spoil his gloating? Jeff clearly didn't believe any of his denials, anyway. Hell, after the impact that sweet, innocent little kiss had had on his system, Mike wasn't sure he believed them himself. Besides, perhaps the rumor of his interest in Melanie would finally get Pam off his case about going out with every available woman she ran across. Maybe that trip to the nursery hadn't been as innocent as he'd believed it to be. Maybe he'd subconsciously known that it would stir up talk, the kind of talk that could save him from all that unwanted matchmaking.

Jeff gave him a knowing look. "You're thinking this will get Pam to stop meddling, aren't you?"

"It crossed my mind," Mike admitted.

"Ha! This kind of rumor is all the motivation she needs to kick her campaign into high gear. You're matrimonial toast, buddy. Accept it now and save yourself a lot of aggravation."

Mike bit back a groan. "Can't you control your wife?"

Jeff gave him a sympathetic look. "You really don't know the first thing about women, do you?"

"No question about that," Mike agreed. "No question at all."

Chapter Five

On Monday night the skies opened up, and the April showers began in earnest. They continued straight through the day on Tuesday and again on Wednesday. Dull gray clouds dumped sheets and sheets of endless, cold rain, turning the yard into a mud bath.

Melanie sat in the dreary kitchen, sipping a cup of tea, eating a freshly baked chocolate chip cookie that was burned on the edges, and regretting that she'd ever agreed to come to Rose Cottage. She was bored. She was lonely. Worst of all, she was daydreaming about yet another man she couldn't have.

There was little question in her mind that, despite his single status, Mike wasn't available. He'd clearly dedicated himself to raising his daughter and maybe to nursing whatever resentments he still felt toward his former wife. The very last thing Melanie needed in her life was a man whose heart wasn't free, whatever the reason.

She ought to pack up and head back to Boston before the appeal of that one kiss made mincemeat of her common sense. She ought to go back, find her dream job, maybe move into a new apartment and definitely throw herself into enough hobbies that she'd forget all about her knack for finding the wrong men. The D'Angelo women had been taught to be independent. She didn't need a man in her life.

Of course, watching the way her parents still got a little gleam in their eyes when they saw each other and their freely given affection with each other had made all of them long to achieve what their parents had. Colleen and Max D'Angelo made marriage look easy.

But even after convincing herself that it was time to go, Melanie reminded herself that it would be a shame to leave Rose Cottage before she finished doing something with her grandmother's garden. She'd studied that photo Mike had found so fascinating, and she was beginning to envision making the yard look like that again. It was the least she could do in her grandmother's memory.

Of course, if the rains kept up like this, it would be summer before the ground dried up enough for her to get the first flower planted. Melanie wanted to be back home before that, making plans, embarking on her new life.

She bit into another too-crisp cookie, then tossed it aside in disgust. If only she had Maggie's talent in the kitchen. Instead, she was an absolute disaster. Who else could manage to destroy slice-and-bake cookies?

Her pity party was in full swing when someone knocked on the front door, startling her. Melanie was so relieved by the prospect of a distraction, she practically ran to the door, then faltered when she glanced through the window and spotted a dripping-wet Mike and Jessie on the porch. The little twinge of excitement that formed low in her belly was a warning. She was way too eager to see these two. A smart woman would leave the door firmly closed.

Since she tended to listen to her heart, not her head, she opened the door. "Did you two come by boat?" she asked, standing aside to let them in. Jessie clung to her father's hand and regarded Melanie silently.

Mike grinned. "You sound edgy. Getting a little cabin fever?"

"Something like that," she admitted. "Hi, Jessie."

Jessie peered up at her and finally smiled. "Hi."

"I thought for a minute a cat had got your tongue," Melanie teased.

Jessie looked perplexed. "There's no cat here."

Melanie chuckled. "No, there's not. It's just an expression. Here, let me take your coats. Can I get you something hot to drink? Maybe some hot chocolate, Jessie?"

At last Jessie gave her a full-fledged smile. "I love hot chocolate. So does Daddy."

Melanie met his gaze. "Is that so?" she asked him as she led the way into the kitchen. She hung their coats on the drying pegs beside the back door, then glanced once more at Mike. The rain had put a bit of wayward curl into his hair, which gave him a rakish look that was even more appealing.

"Are you sure you wouldn't prefer coffee or tea?" she asked him.

"Whatever's easiest. We just stopped on the way home from school to make sure you hadn't floated away."

"As you can see, I'm still here. Since I finished up

most of the work I can do inside the house, I've been reduced to baking cookies.'' She gestured toward the plate. ''They're a little overdone, but help yourselves.''

Jessie gave her father a hopeful look. At his nod, she grabbed one and took a bite. Melanie waited for some comment about the burned edges, but Jessie climbed onto a kitchen chair and munched happily, seemingly oblivious to the cookie's flaws. Melanie turned to Mike. ''What about you? Are you brave enough to try one? I know they don't look like much.''

He laughed. ''Actually they look a lot like mine— right, Jessie?''

''Uh-huh,'' Jessie said, her mouth full. ''Daddy burns everything.''

''Not everything,'' he protested indignantly, then shrugged. ''I'm great with cereal.''

Melanie laughed. ''Since you have such low expectations, maybe I'll risk inviting you to dinner.''

''Tonight?'' Jessie asked hopefully. ''Daddy was gonna make spaghetti from a can.''

''I definitely think I can improve on that, if you'd like to stay,'' she said, meeting Mike's gaze. ''Maybe real pasta with some garlic bread. Of course, the sauce will be from a jar, but that's still better than canned spaghetti, right?''

''Anything's better than that,'' Mike agreed. ''But if we're staying for dinner, then no more cookies, Jessie. You'll spoil your appetite. Besides, you've already had enough sugar for one afternoon.''

Jessie seemed about to argue, but Mike's steady gaze never wavered and she backed down.

''Can I watch TV?'' she asked instead.

Melanie glanced at Mike for permission. At his nod,

she took Jessie into the living room and left her happily watching a PBS children's show.

"I really only came by to check on you," Mike said, when Melanie got back to the kitchen. "Not to invite ourselves to dinner."

"Believe me, I'm glad of the company," Melanie told him honestly.

"Too much time on your hands to think?" he asked.

"Way too much."

"Want to talk about whatever brought you here? You've listened to me. I'm willing to return the favor."

She shook her head. "It was bad enough wallowing in all that self-pity by myself, I don't want to inflict it on you. I'd rather have you talk to me. Tell me about your latest project or how you ended up here at the end of the earth. You're not from around here, are you?"

"End of the earth?" he inquired. "Isn't that a little bit of an overstatement?"

"It's not Boston."

"But apparently Boston hasn't been all that great to you lately," he reminded her. "Maybe you should think about giving a place like this a chance, instead of dismissing it out of hand."

"I am," she said. "At least for the short term, but I was asking about you. Were you born here?"

"No. I came from Richmond. I actually started my business there, but when Linda and I split up, I realized Jessie and I needed to get away, not just to put some distance between us and my ex-wife, but so I wouldn't be so consumed with work that I couldn't spend enough time with Jessie."

"What made you pick this area?"

"It's beautiful. It's near the water. There's a lot of building going on, so there's a need for a good landscape designer. It's not that far from home, so Jessie can see her grandparents from time to time. It's been a good fit. I like being part of a small, growing community.''

"Had you been here before, or did you just drive around till you found a place that suited you?''

"Actually I have a friend who's in the nursery business here, Jeff Clayborne.''

"That was his nursery we went to the other day,'' Melanie recalled.

"Exactly. He was out on a job, or you would have met him.'' He gave her a rueful look. "Actually he's heard all about you.''

She regarded him with surprise. "Really?''

"Word travels fast around here. When I saw him Monday, Jeff had already heard about Jessie and me being at the nursery, the ice cream shop and the bookstore with a gorgeous woman. I'm pretty sure he's up to speed on your entire family history by now, too.''

"Now, there's one of the obvious disadvantages of small town living, don't you think? Everyone knows your business.''

Mike shrugged. "Seems to me like gossip gets around in a big city, too—at least to your own family and circle of friends and business associates.''

Melanie thought of how a fear of gossip had sent her scurrying out of Boston and realized he was exactly right. "I guess 'good' gossip does circulate wherever you are,'' she agreed.

"So, what do people back in Boston say about you?'' he asked.

"Hard to tell,'' Melanie said evasively. "I try not to give them much to talk about.''

"You told me once before that there's no special man in your life, right?''

"None," she said tightly.

He studied her closely. "Something tells me there's a story behind that. You're too beautiful to be alone."

"I was with the wrong man. It ended. That's the whole story."

"In a nutshell," he conceded. "Someday I'd like to hear the unabridged version."

"Why?"

"Isn't that what friends do? Tell each other their deep, dark secrets?"

She laughed. "*Girl* friends might do that. I'm not sure I've ever shared my deep dark secrets with a guy. What about you? Do you pour out your secrets to, say, Brenda?"

"Not exactly. Not that she hasn't tried to pry them out of me. And Jeff's wife, Pam, is a master at the poking and prodding game. Her degree's in horticulture, but you'd think she graduated magna cum laude in investigative reporting."

"How does that make you feel?"

"Edgy," he admitted. "Uncomfortable."

Melanie smiled. "There you go. That's exactly how your poking around makes me feel. Why don't we move on? We could discuss whether or not you're any good at all at making a salad."

Mike looked as if he might argue, but then he gave her a chagrined smile. "Whatever you want. I happen to be excellent at making salad. There's no cooking involved."

"Perfect," she said. "And Jessie can set the table."

Mike opened his mouth, no doubt to argue, but Melanie cut him off. "The dishes are old. If she drops something, it's no big deal."

"Then by all means, let her set the table," he relented.

Melanie regarded him curiously. "Doesn't she have chores at home?"

"Sure. She makes her own bed. It's not pretty, but she does it. And I'm teaching her to do laundry. We're a little shaky on the sorting process, which is why I'm sometimes wearing pink underwear."

"I'd like to see that," Melanie said without thinking.

He gave her an amused look. "Oh, really?"

She frowned at the glint in his eyes. "You know what I meant."

"Of course I do," he said, though he couldn't seem to stop grinning. He stood up. "Where's the salad stuff?"

"I generally keep my salad 'stuff' in the refrigerator. How about you?" Melanie teased.

He scowled at her. "I meant the bowl you want to use."

"Ah, that would be in the cupboard over here," she said.

But just as she opened the cabinet door, Mike stepped in behind her and reached over her head. She could feel the press of his legs along the backs of her thighs. His hips cradled her derriere. The intimacy sent a wave of longing washing over her, to say nothing of the kind of heat she'd sworn to avoid.

He set the bowl on the counter in front of her but didn't back away. Instead, he sighed.

"I swore I wasn't going to do this again," he murmured just before he pressed a kiss to the side of her neck. "Damn, but you smell good. I couldn't get this scent out of my head all day after I kissed you on Monday. It about drove me crazy."

Melanie trembled, as much from the helpless dismay she heard in his voice as from the touch of his lips on her skin. She knew precisely how he felt, understood exactly what it was like to have sworn off something only to be unable to resist it.

In fact, she was clinging to the counter with white-knuckled determination right now to keep from turning in Mike's arms and transforming that tender kiss into something filled with heat and urgency. There was no mistaking the press of his arousal against her or the wanting in his voice. She understood all of that, too.

Slowly, inevitably—and all too soon—he backed away.

"I'm sorry," he muttered, avoiding her gaze.

Melanie had lived with too many regrets for too long now. She didn't want another one—her own or his—on her conscience. "Don't be," she said harshly. "We're both adults here. Sometimes things just happen. The only mistake would be in making too much of it."

He faced her then. "Just a kiss, right?"

It was like equating an earthquake with a little shiver, but still she nodded. "Just a kiss."

He smiled, his eyes smoldering in a way that told her he understood the depth of the lie as well as she did.

"Maybe we'd better get Jessie in here now," he suggested. "Before I get any other bright ideas."

Melanie laughed and the intense moment was broken...for now.

Mike had never thought of himself as the type to play with fire, but apparently he'd been mistaken. He was playing with a whole damned inferno when it came to being around Melanie. She could send him up in flames in a heartbeat.

He told himself it was only because he'd been a celibate saint since he'd moved to town. After all this time, it was perfectly natural to assume that sooner or later some woman was going to set him off.

Unfortunately, it just happened to be a woman who was hurting and vulnerable, rather than someone like the very willing Brenda, who could fend for herself. If he took advantage of the chemistry between him and Melanie and wound up hurting her, he'd feel like a first-class jerk. And if he let her into his life, already knowing she was going to run out on him in the end, it would prove him to be an even bigger jerk.

That meant he ought to be steering clear of her, avoiding her like the plague, maybe finding some new route to get to work that wouldn't take him directly past Melanie's house every morning and night. Instead, he punished himself for his wayward thoughts by driving by Rose Cottage and testing his willpower.

Since he appeared intent on pulling into her driveway not two days after lecturing himself on avoiding her, apparently his willpower sucked almost as much as his judgment.

Mike slogged through the mud, telling himself he wouldn't stay long. He'd tell her that it was still too wet to plant the flowers they'd picked up last weekend, despite the sliver of sun that had finally worked its way through the clouds on Thursday afternoon and seemed to be struggling against this morning's gloom as well. Then he'd leave. No big deal.

Famous last words.

He found her outside whacking at the rosebushes with an oversize pair of hedge clippers and a deadly gleam in her eyes. The sight of it horrified him on so many levels it had him tearing across the lawn to snatch the clippers away from her before she did any more damage.

She stared at him as if he'd gone mad. ''Why'd you

do that?'' she demanded indignantly. ''Aren't you the one who's been carrying on about getting these bushes under control?''

He barely contained a groan. ''Under control, not murdered in their sleep.''

She scowled at him. ''I'm not murdering the damn bushes. I'm trimming them back.''

''Heaven save me from amateurs,'' he murmured. ''Where are your garden tools?''

''In the shed over there,'' she conceded grudgingly, then followed him when he stalked off in that direction, still muttering.

''Whatever you're saying about me, say it so I can hear it,'' she said.

''You don't want to hear this,'' he retorted, yanking open the door and staring at the excellent collection of gardening implements. It was yet more testimony that Cornelia Lindsey had been an expert gardener who'd cared for the tools she used as well as she had for the garden itself.

''Ever heard of dusting?'' he grumbled, as he found some first-class pruning shears.

Melanie glowered at him. ''In the house. Not in a tool shed.''

''The same rules apply.'' He shook his head. ''Never mind. Just come with me. Try not to get in my way.''

''If you're this charming when you're teaching Jessie, I'm not surprised she rebels,'' Melanie said.

There was a little too much truth in the observation, so Mike chose to ignore it. Instead, he led the way to the rosebush Melanie had been attacking. ''Watch and learn,'' he said as he began gently shaping the bush, snipping carefully so it would flourish, not wither and die.

"Why is that one bit different from what I was doing?" Melanie asked after watching him awhile. "It's just going to take longer."

He rolled his eyes. "It's one of those times when patience will be rewarded. If you chop at it the way you were doing, you'll destroy it. See here? There's new growth. And here."

He showed her the markers he was using in making each careful cut. When he'd trimmed one entire bush, he handed the pruning shears to her. "Your turn."

She accepted the shears gingerly, then frowned at the bush. She immediately reached for a branch and was about to lop it off, when he winced.

"What?" she demanded, shooting him a look of disgust. "It's dead."

"Not entirely. Look again." He pointed to a nodule that would eventually produce new leaves. "See? If you cut above that, the new leaves will appear anyday now."

"This is going to take forever," she said, but she diligently cut where he'd told her to. "What about this branch?"

He grinned. "You tell me."

She bent over to study it, giving him a very nice view of her lovely derriere. He was so absorbed he almost missed the quizzical look she was giving him as she pointed out where she thought she ought to cut.

"Looks good to me," he said, enjoying the flash of triumph in her eyes. It was almost as bright as the sun that was finally beating down from a clear, blue sky.

She'd made several more careful snips without any need for his interference before she finally turned and frowned at him. "You could help, you know."

"I am helping."

"How?"

"I'm supervising. Without me watching over you, who knows how much damage you might do?"

"Very funny. How many rosebushes do you suppose there are in the yard?" she asked plaintively, wiping the perspiration from her brow and leaving behind a streak of dirt.

Mike had to work hard to resist the desire to brush away that streak on her forehead.

"Enough to keep you out of trouble for a good long while," he said cheerfully. "How about some iced tea? Now that the sun's back out, it's hot out here."

"I'm surprised you noticed, since you're standing around in the shade doing nothing."

He ignored the sarcasm. "Keep at it. I'll bring you a sandwich along with your tea."

"You trust me enough to leave me alone for ten whole minutes?" She feigned shock.

"Thirty actually. I'm going to pick up lunch in town." He gave her a stern look. "And no sitting down on the job the minute my back is turned. I expect one more bush trimmed when I get back."

"It's my damned yard!" she shouted after him.

He laughed. "I know. That's why you're doing the work."

The one good thing about keeping her good and mad at him, he decided as he headed into town to pick up lunch, was that even if he was tempted to kiss her, she'd probably slug him and pretty much destroy the impulse.

"You're mean and arrogant and controlling," Melanie accused as she sat next to Mike in the swing in the backyard, reveling in the welcome breeze off the bay. "I think I could hate you."

"That's nice," he murmured, not sounding especially

distressed by the charges. He glanced sideways at her. "The yard's starting to look good, though, don't you think so?"

Melanie could barely turn around to follow the direction of his gaze. Every muscle in her body ached, including a few she hadn't been aware of having. She tried to view it through his eyes. All she saw were a bunch of stubby-looking rosebushes. There were at least as many that were still growing out of control.

"Are you sure they're going to grow back?" she asked. "Right now they just look denuded."

He laughed. "They'll grow back. You'll have so many roses later this summer, the scent out here will overwhelm you."

She regarded the garden wistfully. "Too bad I won't be here for that."

"Stay," he said, not sure why he was so determined to change her mind when he knew the risks involved to his own peace of mind.

"I've already told you that I can't."

"No," he said with exaggerated patience. "You told me you *won't,* not that you *can't.*"

"Same difference."

"Not really. One's a choice you're making."

Melanie sighed. It was true. She was making a choice to go back to Boston, but it was the only choice. That was home, and eventually she did have to go back there. This was an interlude, nothing more.

As if to prove that peaceful moments like this couldn't last, the silence was split by the sound of a powerful car engine, then the cutting of the motor and an eruption of laughter.

"Oh, my God," she murmured, recognizing first Ashley's voice, then Maggie's, then Jo's.

Mike regarded her with consternation. "What?"

"My sisters," she said, aware that she sounded as if disaster were about to strike. "They didn't tell me they were coming."

Amusement flickered in Mike's eyes. "And that's a problem because what? There are no clean sheets on the beds?"

"You know perfectly well that's not the issue," she grumbled, jumping out of the swing as if it were on fire. "I need to get out there before they…" Her voice trailed off.

"Before they see me?" he pressed.

"Yes, if you must know."

"Ashamed of me?" he pressed, his expression suggesting the remark wasn't made entirely in jest.

"Don't be absurd. It's just that they'll make too much of you being here."

He laughed. "So?"

"You don't know my sisters," she said grimly. "Stick around and you'll see exactly the kind of inquisition of which they're capable. You think Pam asks a lot of questions? Have I mentioned that Ashley is a highly successful criminal defense attorney? She never loses. She could cross-examine anyone and get them to admit to things they'd never even *considered* doing."

"Ah, I think I'm starting to catch your drift. You think they'll take one look at you and me, all sweaty and flushed, and assume we've been up to something besides gardening," he said in a deliberately provocative way that made her palms sweat.

"Exactly," she murmured, her throat suddenly dry.

He bent down and gave her a hard kiss that took her breath away. When he released her, she swayed.

"Why the hell did you do that? Didn't you hear anything I said?"

"Every word," he said, sauntering off just as Ashley, Maggie and Jo emerged from the house. "I figured since they were already staring out the window, they might as well get the whole show."

Melanie clenched her fists at her side. "You're a pig," she shouted after him.

He merely waved and went on, leaving her to deal with the fallout. He really was a pig, albeit an incredibly sexy one.

Melanie sighed, then sucked in a deep breath and prepared to face her sisters.

Chapter Six

"Here for three weeks and she's already met the sexiest hunk in the entire Northern Neck," Jo taunted Melanie Friday night after Mike had disappeared around a corner of the house.

"Sexy?" Melanie asked innocently, determined to minimize Mike's attributes, determined not to get drawn into any discussion about him at all. "I hadn't noticed."

"Oh, God, Jeremy blinded her," Maggie lamented. "She's ruined for life."

"Worse, he robbed her of all feeling," Jo added. "If a man kissed me the way that guy just kissed Melanie, I guarantee I'd understand the meaning of *sexy*. Who is he, by the way? Just in case I happen to bump into him while we're in town, I want to be able to greet him by name and check out his kissing technique for myself."

Melanie felt Ashley's curious gaze on her, but avoided meeting her big sister's eyes. Ashley had always been able to read her better than the others. She fought to keep a perfectly neutral expression on her face.

"His name is Stefan Mikelewski, but he prefers to be called Mike," she said grudgingly. "And if you do happen to run into him in town, I expect you to cross the street, if need be, to avoid him. You're not to take it upon yourselves to cross-examine him, and you *most certainly* are not to experiment with kissing him."

Jo laughed, looking triumphant. "Thought so. She is so into the guy."

Melanie tried to ignore the teasing. "Why are all three of you here?" she grumbled. "I thought you were going to take turns. I also thought maybe you'd actually let me know you were coming."

Ashley grinned. "Something you have to hide, sis? Say, a new relationship? Your protests so far are not all that convincing."

Melanie glared at her big sister. "No, I do not have anything to hide, but there's not enough food in the house to feed you guys and, frankly, I could have used a little fortification before facing even one of you, much less all three of you at once."

"We decided you'd only tell us you were just fine and try to put us off if we called first," Maggie told her. "Besides, Ashley wound up a court case yesterday, so she needed a break. I finished the food spread for the July issue of the magazine, so I was ready for a change, too. And you know Jo—she'll go anywhere, anytime."

"Are you saying I'm easy?" Jo inquired testily.

"No, we're saying you're energetic and fun," Ashley soothed.

"Now, Mel, tell us all about the handsome Mr. Mikelewski who just snuck out of here to avoid meeting us."

"There's nothing to tell," Melanie insisted. "And he didn't sneak out. He was already on his way out when you arrived."

"Yeah, I always try to steam up the windows right before I walk out the door, figuratively speaking," Ashley commented dryly. "You mean there's nothing you want to share with us."

"I mean I don't know anything about him except that he's a landscape designer and he's livid that we neglected grandmother's garden. I've taken more grief from that man than I have from anyone in my life, with the possible exception of Jeremy the scoundrel."

"Is this Mike divorced? Married? Children? You don't know any of that?" Ashley asked, looking horrified.

"He's a single dad, and his daughter's a bit of a handful," Melanie replied, realizing that she was not going to get out of giving them a few tidbits about Mike to chew on. Otherwise they'd pester her to death or, worse, track Mike down for the answers they were after.

"Where's his wife?"

"I have no idea. He doesn't say much about her. She's not here, I do know that much." She was not going to tell them about the addiction. It was none of their business. It certainly wasn't her story to share.

"Are you sure he's not carrying the torch for the ex?" Maggie asked.

"I'm relatively sure of that much," Melanie said. The real issue was whether he'd ever get past the resentment he felt toward the woman who'd put his daughter's life at risk. "Although I suspect he still has some issues to work out."

"Relatively sure? Issues?" Maggie echoed, looking dismayed. "You need to ask the man about these issues.

Don't leave anything to chance, Melanie. Not again. Otherwise you're liable to get in over your head the same way you did with Jeremy, then find out you missed some important truths."

"Didn't you hear me? Not if I assume there are unresolved issues between them. That's warning enough for me," Melanie retorted. At least it should be. However, every time Mike kissed her, the warning bells dimmed just a little, until now she could barely hear them.

"But then you might be losing out on the best single, totally available man in the region," Jo countered.

"Not interested," Melanie said firmly.

"Uh-huh," all three of her sisters chorused skeptically.

"Blind and dumb," Ashley added.

Melanie scowled at the lot of them. "Pizza or crab cakes?" she asked testily. "I'm starving."

For a moment she thought her mention of food had fallen on deaf ears, but eventually Ashley took the hint.

"Crab, by all means," Ashley said, then had to spoil it by adding, "and then a few more answers about the intriguing Mr. Mikelewski for dessert."

Mike was still distracted when he picked Jessie up at school. He couldn't seem to shake the feeling that he'd made a mistake kissing Melanie and then leaving her to explain things to her sisters, especially since she was already afraid they'd make too much of finding him there.

"Daddy, you're not paying attention," Jessie accused.

"What? Sorry, baby."

"I said I got an A on my reading test. The teacher

said I was way ahead of everybody else in class. That's 'cause you and me read every night.''

He gave her his full attention. ''That's because you work very hard at it,'' he told her. ''I am so proud of you. This deserves a celebration—what would you like to do tonight?''

''See Melanie,'' she said at once. ''I want to tell her about my test.''

''We'll have to do that another time,'' he said. ''She has company.''

Jessie's face clouded over. ''What kind of company?''

''Her sisters surprised her this afternoon. They came all the way from Boston to visit.''

''We could still go,'' Jessie said, her expression determined.

''Not tonight. We'll tell her about the test on Monday, after they're gone.''

''But I want to go *now!*''

Mike lost patience. ''Jessica Marie, stop that right this second, or we won't celebrate anything.''

She immediately fell silent, but a single huge tear rolled down her cheek. Mike was instantly assailed by guilt and the desire to take back his sharp words, but he settled on another tack.

''I'm sorry you're disappointed,'' he said quietly. ''What about going out to dinner? We could go to the crab shanty and get a dozen crabs.''

''I don't like crabs,'' Jessie grumbled.

Mike had to struggle once again to hang on to his patience. ''You do too like crabs. They're your favorite, especially when you get to pick out the crabmeat yourself. You love hitting them with that mallet.''

''Well, I don't want to do that tonight,'' she said stubbornly.

Mike could see in her eyes that she desperately wanted to give in and say yes, but she would rather spoil her evening than say yes, now that she'd dug in her heels. He knew a lot about stubborn pride. It was a trait they shared.

"Okay," he said at last, coming up with a way to make it easier for her to give in. "Then you can sit there while I eat. If you're not hungry, you don't have to eat a thing."

"But it's *my* celebration," she protested.

He shrugged. "It's up to you," he said, pulling into the parking lot of the waterfront seafood restaurant that specialized in casual dining. It was a favorite of theirs because no one cared how messy Jessie was. No one could pick crabs neatly.

As soon as they entered, Lena Jensen greeted them with a huge smile. Lena had been running the place for her brother for thirty years. There wasn't a person in town she didn't know and very little gossip that didn't reach her ears.

"It's about time you came to see me, young lady," she scolded Jessie. "I've missed you. Heard you did real well on a reading test today."

Jessie's eyes turned round. "How did you know?"

Lena winked at Mike. "My grandson's in your class," she reminded Jessie. "Not much at school or around town I don't hear about." She gave Mike a pointed look. "Heard you've been helping out over at Cornelia Lindsey's cottage. That granddaughter of hers is a looker, isn't she? At least, that's what everyone is saying. I remember Cornelia bringing all those girls in when they were young. Can't say I recall which was which, but all four of them were real beauties. It's Melanie who's here, is that right?"

Mike had only caught a glimpse of the others this afternoon, but it had been enough to know that Lena was exactly right. Each one was gorgeous. "Actually they're all here. The others arrived this afternoon for a visit."

"Well, isn't that nice?" Lena said. "I imagine they'll be in before too long. This was the first place they came whenever they hit town to visit their grandmother. It was a tradition I doubt they'll break."

Mike bit back a groan. He hoped she was wrong about that. Melanie would not be pleased to find him here.

"Daddy, are we gonna eat? I'm hungry."

He glanced down into Jessie's upturned face. All traces of her moodiness had vanished. "Lena, you can forget about the menus. Put in an order for a dozen steamed crabs for us, one soda and a beer. It's a nice night. We'll find our way to a table on the deck."

"I'll get the order in right now," Lena said. "You're in luck. It's still early in the season, so supplies are low, but we got in some beauties this morning."

Mike and Jessie made their way to the outdoor deck and chose a table with a good view of the mallards and gulls on the water. In another hour or two, the deck would be packed with locals and tourists, here for the excellent food and the spectacular sunset reflected off the inlet from the bay.

For now, though, Mike and Jessie had it to themselves. Lena brought their drinks, then hurried back to greet the next batch of customers.

"Daddy, do you think that duck is lonely?" Jessie asked plaintively, pointing to a female mallard drifting on the water apart from the others.

Mike gave the question the serious consideration Jessie expected before shaking his head. "No, I figure she's just taking a break. She's probably been pestered all day long and needs some time to herself.''

Jessie nodded, her expression thoughtful. ''That's what I think, too.''

Mike studied his daughter closely and realized that she still wasn't entirely satisfied. Something else was clearly on her mind. ''Something bothering you, kiddo?''

''I was thinking,'' she began, regarding him earnestly, ''it would be fun to have sisters.''

Mike gulped. ''Really? What on earth put that idea into your head?''

''Melanie has sisters. You and Miss Lena said so. And my friends at school have sisters and brothers, too. Sometimes they're pests, but sometimes a pest is better than not having anybody around.''

''Are you lonely?'' he asked, his heart in his throat. He'd convinced himself that they didn't need anything more than what they had—each other. ''I thought Lyssa Clayborne was your best friend. You two arguing or something?''

''Friends are different. They don't live with you,'' his daughter explained.

''Then you *are* lonely,'' Mike concluded.

As if she sensed that she had somehow hurt his feelings, Jessie shook her head. ''I'm just saying sisters would be fun—better than brothers, probably, but brothers would be okay, too.''

He grinned at her. ''You think there's a store where we can pick out a few?''

''No, Daddy!'' she protested, giggling. ''You can't buy sisters.''

''Oh, right,'' Mike said. ''I forgot.''

''No, you didn't. You were teasing me.''

"Only because I like hearing you laugh," he said. "Sorry I can't be more help when it comes to the sister thing."

"That's okay," Jessie said, sounding resigned. "Maybe someday we'll get a mom and some sisters."

Eyes stinging, Mike turned away. It was thoroughly frustrating to discover that he couldn't give his child one of the few things she really wanted. Feeling inadequate, he looked up just in time to spot Melanie and her sisters emerging onto the deck. She spotted him and halted in her tracks.

"Maybe we should sit inside. It's cool out here," he heard her tell her siblings, trying to jostle them back through the door.

Unfortunately, one of her sisters caught a glimpse of him and realized exactly what Melanie was up to.

"Oh, no, you don't," she said to Melanie. "Perhaps we can join your friend and his daughter."

She was past Melanie and across the deck before Melanie could react. Hand outstretched, she greeted Mike. "Hi, I'm Ashley D'Angelo, Melanie's older sister. And this is Jo. Maggie's back there, trying to convince Melanie that it's too late to run."

Mike grinned. "And why would she feel the need to run?" he asked, though it was perfectly obvious from the curious glint in her big sister's sharp, intelligent eyes.

"You tell me," Ashley suggested. "Maybe it has something to do with that kiss we caught when you knew we were watching."

"Were you?" Mike asked innocently. "I had no idea."

Ashley laughed. "You'd make a lousy witness, Mr. Mikelewski. You get this little tic at the corner of your eye when you lie."

He deliberately rubbed his eye. "Must have gotten something in it. There's a lot of pollen around. Maybe you should sit inside."

"Not a chance," she said, already maneuvering another table over to theirs. She frowned at him. "You could help with this."

He shook his head. "I'm waiting for my cue from Melanie. She seems reluctant for this to happen."

"She doesn't trust me not to go poking around into your personal business," Ashley said unrepentantly. "She'll get over it."

He laughed, liking her honesty. "Frankly, I'm not sure I trust you, either. She says you're hell on wheels in a courtroom cross-examination."

Ashley gave her sister a long, considering look. "Did she really? I wonder why she'd do that. I guess I'll just have to work that much harder to catch you off guard, now that I know you've been forewarned."

Melanie arrived in time to overhear the last and groaned. "Could we please sit somewhere else?" she begged, giving a look of silent apology to Mike.

"Not on my account," he said. "Besides, Jessie is bursting to tell you her news. She wanted to come by a little while ago, but I talked her into coming here to celebrate instead."

All four women turned their eyes on Jessie, then. She squirmed under all that sudden scrutiny, and for a moment, Mike thought her shyness would get the better of her. But then Melanie pulled out the chair beside her, and Jessie immediately scrambled into her lap.

"Guess what?" she said excitedly, her gaze on Melanie's face.

"What?"

"I got an A on my reading test. Isn't that the best news ever?"

"That is fantastic news," Melanie agreed. "In fact, it might be the very best news I've heard in a long time. No wonder you're celebrating."

"Daddy's getting crabs so we can hit 'em with a mallet."

Maggie chuckled. "Sounds energetic."

Mike met her gaze. "You have no idea. The safest seat is at that end of the table, as far from Jessie as you can get."

Jessie's gaze was intent on Melanie's face. "Are these your sisters?"

Melanie nodded and introduced them.

"I was telling Daddy that I wish I had sisters," Jessie announced. "And a mom."

Mike choked on the sip of beer he'd just taken. "Yes, well, we all have our impossible dreams," he said, as three women studied him with absolutely fascinated expressions. Melanie merely looked as if she'd like to crawl under the table.

"What's so impossible about that?" Ashley inquired, regarding him intently.

Melanie scowled at her sister. "Leave the man alone, Ashley. He's not on trial."

"Just curious," Ashley said. "Aren't *you?*"

"No, I am not," Melanie said firmly.

"Ha!" The chorus came from Jo and Maggie.

"If you all don't behave, I'm leaving you here to walk home," Melanie threatened.

Ashley grinned. "It might be worth it."

"Yeah, we'd have Mike all to ourselves," Jo agreed. "Who knows what secrets we could pry out of him?"

Melanie turned to Mike. "Ignore them. I love them,

but they're pains in the butt. They have absolutely no idea of boundaries when it comes to social conversation. It's a trait they picked up from our father. Since it drove all of us nuts when he did it, you'd think they'd know better.''

He laughed. "I think I can handle your sisters."

This time she was the one who muttered, ''Ha!''

To prove his point, he turned to Ashley, who was clearly the leader of the pack. ''Tell me, how's your social life these days?''

''As if she has time for one,'' Maggie murmured.

''Ah, not so hot?'' Mike guessed, picking up on the comment. ''I have some friends I could introduce you to while you're here. They're a little rough around the edges, but I imagine you could whip them into shape in no time.''

''I'm not here looking for a project,'' Ashley said haughtily. ''If I wanted someone in my life, I'm sure I could find a suitable candidate in Boston.''

He chuckled. ''If I didn't know better, I'd say that sounded downright snobbish, Ms. D'Angelo. Something wrong with a blue-collar guy?''

''Not as long as it's an Italian-silk-blend blue collar,'' Maggie taunted.

Ashley frowned at her. ''I am not a snob,'' she said, promptly rising to the bait.

''But a blue-collar guy wouldn't suit you, isn't that what you just said?''

''No. I said…'' Her voice trailed off. ''Oh, never mind. You're only doing this to prove you can hold your own. You don't give two hoots about my social life.''

''Sure I do,'' Mike insisted. ''You're Melanie's sister. I want you to be happy.''

"And Melanie?" Ashley asked tartly. "Are you try-ing to make sure she's happy, too?"

"Doing my best," he said easily. "Of course, she'd be a lot happier if I stopped pestering her about getting that garden at Rose Cottage into shape, right, Melanie?"

"Absolutely," she said at once. "In fact, now that my sisters are here, why don't you make them help? They're as much at fault as I am for the disaster the garden's become."

"Good idea," he said at once. "What time should I be there in the morning? Say, six? It should be just about daylight then. With all of you working in the garden, we can get the job done in no time. I hope none of you mind getting your hands dirty."

Ashley glanced at her perfectly manicured nails, then stared at him in horror. "Not a chance, Mr. Mikelewski. Besides, isn't Melanie paying you to take care of the garden?"

"Nope. I'm a volunteer supervisor."

Surprise registered in Ashley's eyes. "Is that so? And this is your profession, landscape design?"

"That's right."

"Then why would you offer your services for noth-ing?" she asked. "What exactly are you expecting in return?"

"A garden that looks like it did in its heyday," he said simply. "That's my only mission."

"Told you," Melanie muttered to her sisters.

Oddly enough, she didn't look especially pleased to have whatever she'd told them confirmed. Mike figured he'd think about that later. For right now, it was enough to know that he'd apparently thrown the skeptical, in-quisitive Ashley off the scent.

"Then what was that kiss about?" Ashley demanded. "Don't you dare toy with her."

"Ashley, that's enough," Melanie said, blushing furiously.

"It most certainly is not enough," Ashley retorted. "I won't allow this man to take advantage of you."

"Don't yell at my daddy," Jessie whispered, catching all of them by surprise.

Ashley immediately looked chagrined. "Sweetie, I am so sorry. I didn't mean to yell at him."

Jessie regarded her skeptically. "Then why did you?"

"I lost my head for a minute, that's all."

"Where'd it go?" Jessie asked, drawing a laugh that broke the tension.

"Hard to say," Ashley told her. "But I promise I won't open my mouth again till I find it."

That drew the biggest chorus of hoots yet from her sisters.

Mike couldn't help getting a kick out of them. They were all so damned protective of Melanie, yet so straightforward and blunt with each other. He admired that kind of honesty and loyalty. With no brothers or sisters of his own, he'd never experienced anything quite like it. He'd hoped to find it in his marriage, but look how that had turned out.

"No need to stay quiet on my account," he told Ashley. "I can take whatever you want to dish out, as long as you're not afraid of Jessie. She's as protective of me as you are of your sisters. It's not a bad trait to have."

Ashley met his gaze, then slowly nodded. "You'll do," she said at last.

Mike faltered at the note of approval in her voice. What the hell had just happened here? Had Ashley given him her blessing? He gazed around the table to see three women regarding him solemnly and one looking as if she'd rather be anywhere else on the planet.

He didn't want Ashley's damn blessing. That implied that he was seriously interested in a relationship with Melanie, which he absolutely was not. Not that kind of a relationship, anyway.

And the kind he was interested in—hot, passionate and fleeting—was definitely not in the cards.

A part of him wanted to make all of that very clear, so there would be no misunderstandings, but he valued his life too much. He could just hear himself explaining that he only did casual flings and finding himself tossed straight over the railing of this deck. It wouldn't be pretty.

"Maybe we should change the subject," Melanie suggested firmly.

"To what?" Ashley asked, her gaze still steady on Mike.

"Something safer and less controversial," Melanie said. "Say, politics or religion."

Mike stared at her and realized she was perfectly serious. Or desperate. He could relate to that. The truth was, right this instant, surrounded by D'Angelo women and a daughter who'd just announced a need for a mom, he was feeling pretty damn desperate himself.

Chapter Seven

"That was interesting," Ashley declared when they'd returned from dinner and her unexpected opportunity to grill Mike. "Let's have ice cream and discuss what we found out about the intriguing Mr. Mikelewski."

"Let's not," Melanie said, wishing for the moment that she'd been an only child. Having sisters wasn't always all it was cracked up to be, especially sisters who thought they had a God-given right to meddle. "We were all there. We heard every word you and Mike exchanged. I don't think we need to do a postconversation analysis like those TV guys who feel a need to dissect a presidential speech the entire nation has just heard."

"But there's a lot to be learned from comparing notes, seeing if we all got the same impression," Ashley insisted. "That's what makes the jury system so effective."

"Now the three of you have turned into a jury?" Melanie asked. "That's comforting."

"No, I only meant that two heads are better than one, or in our case four heads," Ashley replied.

"Make that three. You all can compare notes to your heart's content. I'm going to bed." Melanie headed for the stairs. "And by the way, your beds aren't made. You'll have to do that yourselves. The clean sheets are in the closet. Try not to wake me."

"Do you get the feeling she's not happy with us?" Ashley asked before Melanie had hit the bottom step.

"*You,*" Jo and Maggie replied. "She's not happy with *you.*"

"*Me?* What did I do?"

Melanie leaned against the wall and grinned as she eavesdropped. Ashley really was oblivious to the fallout when she was on a self-righteous mission. She expected everyone to see that she had their best interests at heart, no matter how intrusive her behavior.

"Let's start with embarrassing her in front of her new friend," Jo explained patiently.

"And making more of this relationship than either she or Mike thinks there is," Maggie added. "How would you like it if we spotted you having lunch with some casual acquaintance and then plopped ourselves down at the table and proceeded to cross-examine him?"

"You'd never do that," Ashley declared confidently.

"No, we wouldn't, but that is what you do," Jo said. "It really can be annoying. Melanie got it just right at dinner. Remember how we hated it when Dad did that to our dates? You're even worse. You've got all that hard-ass courtroom experience going for you. If you ask me, Mike held up pretty well. I'm just surprised he didn't deck you. If it had been me on the receiving end of that interrogation, I might have.''

''Seriously?'' Ashley asked, sounding genuinely perplexed by their assessment.

''Yes, seriously,'' Jo and Maggie confirmed.

''Oh, God,'' Ashley moaned. ''I am so sorry. I'd better go tell her.''

Melanie barely made it to the top of the steps before she heard her sister coming after her. She dove into bed and pulled the covers up to her chin.

Ashley appeared in the doorway. ''Mel, you asleep?''

''What?'' Melanie replied, injecting a note of grogginess into her voice.

''Oh, stop it,'' Ashley said impatiently. ''I know perfectly well you were listening on the steps. I heard you racing to beat me up here.'' She grabbed a corner of the covers and yanked it away to reveal the fact that Melanie was still fully clothed.

Melanie scowled at her. ''If you knew, why'd you bother asking if I was asleep?'' she grumbled.

''I had high hopes that you'd be honest with me.''

''It was a test?'' Melanie asked incredulously.

''I thought it might indicate if you would be willing to tell me the truth about what's really going on with you and Mike.''

''I have told you the truth. There is nothing going on. I'm not an idiot, Ashley. I'm only here for a few more weeks at most. Why would I get involved with someone, especially someone with a child who could get hurt if things don't work out?''

''Then you do see all the possible complications and consequences?''

''Of course I do.''

''Just the same, I'd feel a whole lot better if you knew

more about his situation with his ex-wife,'' Ashley said, her brow knit in a worried frown. ''I don't want his unresolved feelings to come back and bite you in the butt.''

''I'm not going to let that happen,'' Melanie assured her. ''Sis, I appreciate your concern, I really do, but give it a rest, okay? Otherwise this is going to be a very long weekend.''

Ashley looked as if she might argue, but she finally sighed and gave Melanie a hug. ''Love you, kid.''

''I love you, too. Now let me get out of these clothes so I can get some sleep. Yard work is damn hard, and Mike maintains a grueling pace. You'll find that out for yourself tomorrow.''

Ashley shuddered. ''I am not working in the yard.''

Filled with a sudden desire for retaliation, Melanie grinned. ''Wanna bet?''

Melanie regarded her three half-asleep sisters with amusement. They were not morning people. That's why she'd deliberately rousted them out of bed at six.

''If you drink your coffee, you'll feel better,'' she assured them. She'd made a very large pot of it. She wafted a cup under Maggie's nose, knowing that the scent of her favorite brew would get to her.

''What the devil's gotten into you?'' Maggie muttered, even as she made a grab for the cup.

''It's revenge,'' Jo said. She frowned at Melanie. ''Isn't it?''

''Let's just say I'm taking advantage of an opportunity that's come my way to share the pleasure of putting this place in order again.''

''Couldn't I just scrub a floor or something, maybe later this afternoon?'' Ashley pleaded, her head resting on her arms on the kitchen table. "It's bad enough that I have to get up at the crack of dawn to be in court, but this is supposed to be a break."

"The floors have been scrubbed and polished," Melanie pointed out. "The walls have been freshly painted. The windows have been washed. This place is a veritable showcase inside, thanks to me. All that's left is the yard and the outside of the house. The house can wait. The yard needs to be done now, according to Mike."

"Where the heck is he? Has he shown up?" Ashley grumbled. "I thought he was the garden drill sergeant. I had no idea he'd designated you to pinch-hit for him."

"If he's smart, he's miles and miles from here," Melanie responded cheerfully. "I am, indeed, taking over for him. Now come on, ladies, let's get busy. All that weeding isn't going to happen by itself. If we finish by lunchtime, I'll take you into town."

"And if we don't?" Maggie asked warily.

"It's grilled cheese sandwiches and canned soup," Melanie told her. "And more weeding this afternoon. I think we're going to need a scythe to get through the overgrown brush down by the water. There are probably snakes in there, too. You're not scared of snakes, are you, Ashley?"

Her big sister gave her a sour look. "You've turned into a mean, vindictive person since you've been here."

Melanie laughed. "Possibly, but I'm feeling better by the minute. I think I'm just about back in control of my life."

"Heaven help us," Ashley muttered, but she got to her feet. "Lead on. Let's get this over with."

Melanie put them to work on the messiest, most exhausting tasks she could think of, then settled into the swing with a cup of coffee. She could see why Mike enjoyed supervising so much. There was something downright relaxing about sitting around with the sun beating down on her shoulders and a good cup of coffee in hand while other people did her bidding.

She wasn't all that surprised when he turned up about nine, glanced around the yard, which was looking about eighty percent improved, and gave her a thumbs-up. "I see you've been busy. Nice work," he said.

"Not me. I'm supervising."

"Who exactly are you supervising?"

She took a quick glance around and realized that her workers had vanished. How had she missed seeing them sneak off?

"Well, they were here," she said with a shrug. "I must have closed my eyes for a minute, and they seized the opportunity to escape. Where's Jessie?"

"Visiting a friend. I thought I'd stop by and see how things were going over here."

"You mean whether they'd let me off the rack?"

He stared at her blankly. "What?"

"Torture," she explained. "They came home last night filled with more questions than ever."

He laughed. "Yes, I imagine they did. Were they satisfied with your answers?"

"No more than they were with yours. I'm hoping to exhaust them, so they'll forget they ever laid eyes on you."

"Has that worked for you?" he asked, his gaze filled with amusement.

"Not so much," she admitted candidly. "But I'm working on it. It's hard, since you keep popping up around here."

"Want me to stay away?"

The offer startled her. "You'd do that?"

"Now that you're actually getting the garden under control, yes." He searched her face. "If that's what you want."

Was it? Melanie honestly didn't know. It was what she *should* want. It was what she'd promised Ashley the night before—that she'd keep things between herself and Mike cool and impersonal. Keeping him away from the house was probably the only way she'd accomplish that, since he had the uncanny ability to get her all hot and bothered even when she was most determined to resist him.

"You probably should keep an eye on things," she said finally. "I could wind up planting hollyhocks on top of daffodils and spoiling everything."

He grinned. "You have a point, but I should probably take off now, before your sisters get back from wherever they're hiding," he said. "No point in getting them all worked up again."

She lifted her gaze to meet his. "I'm sorry they put you through the wringer last night."

"Actually it was kind of fun. Kept me on my toes."

She stared at him. "You enjoyed it?"

"Sure, why not? It was harmless. I like that they're so protective of you. Of course, it's made me wonder why they think you need protecting."

"Long story." She deliberately took a sip of her now-cold coffee and avoided meeting his eyes.

"And you're still not ready to fill me in?"

Melanie wasn't entirely sure why she'd kept quiet, beyond not wanting Mike to lose all respect for her judgment. After all, she had been duped for months by a married man. Yep, that was the reason for her silence, all right. No woman wanted a man to see her for the pathetic idiot she was.

"I doubt I will ever be ready to tell that story to another living soul, especially you," she said honestly. "I'm trying to forget about it."

"Some things you can't forget about until you deal with them," he said.

"The way you've dealt with what Linda did to you and Jessie?"

His expression sobered at once. "Touché," he said grimly. "No more prodding, but I will listen if you ever change your mind, and I won't pass judgment."

"I'll keep that in mind," Melanie said just as her sisters reappeared, showered and looking as fresh and crisp as if they'd never done a lick of work.

"We're ready for lunch," Maggie announced.

"The job's not finished," Melanie pointed out.

"We don't care," Ashley said. "We're going to lunch, anyway. Do you want to come, or do you have better things to do?" She grinned pointedly at Mike.

"Mike was just leaving," Melanie said firmly. "I'll come to lunch with you as long as we stick to a preapproved list of topics."

"Where is this list?" Ashley demanded. "I haven't seen any list." She glanced at Jo and Maggie. "Have you seen a list?"

"I believe it will be easier if you just take note of the one exclusion," Melanie said.

Three pairs of accusing eyes turned toward Mike.

"Hey, it's her rule, not mine," he said. "If a bunch of gorgeous women want to talk about me, I'm okay with it. It'll probably do wonders for my reputation."

"Well, there you go," Ashley said. "No exclusions."

Melanie gave them all a sour look. "We'll discuss this in the car."

"Want me to come along to referee?" Mike inquired.

"No!" four voices chimed emphatically.

Melanie grinned at her sisters. "At least there's one thing we can agree on. Sorry, Mike."

"No problem. I'll just go and track down some of the guys. See what they're saying around town about the D'Angelo sisters."

He sauntered off before any of them could comment.

"Do you think he was serious?" Jo asked, looking surprisingly worried. "Will people be talking about us? About the fact that we're all here?"

"More than likely, especially since we saw Lena last night at the restaurant. She's like a one-woman newscast," Melanie said. "It's no big deal. After all, what could they possibly have to say about us?"

"I'm not very hungry," Jo said. "I think I'll stick around here."

"Jo, you can't do that," Ashley protested.

"I most certainly can," Jo retorted.

"But there's nothing to eat," Melanie reminded her. "We never did get to the store."

"You said there was stuff for grilled cheese sandwiches. That'll do."

Something in Jo's tone told Melanie that she wasn't going to budge. "Okay, sweetie. It's up to you."

"You're going to miss out on pestering Melanie about Mike," Maggie teased.

"Oh, I think you guys can handle that without me," Jo said. "Have fun. Bring home dessert. Something decadent."

She headed for the house before they could take one last shot at arguing with her.

"Any idea what that was about?" Ashley asked, staring after her worriedly.

"None," Melanie said.

"Oh, well, Maggie and I can gang up on her on the way home," Ashley said. "Let's concentrate on you for now. Organizing one sister's life at a time is all I can handle."

"And we thought you prided yourself on multitasking," Maggie commented.

"A law practice is not nearly as complicated as Melanie's life," Ashley explained breezily.

"Let's leave my life alone, too," Melanie retorted. "Or I'll be staying here with Jo."

Her sisters determinedly linked arms with her.

"Not a chance," Maggie said.

Ashley grinned at her. "It'll be painless. We promise."

Judging from the glint in her eyes, she was lying through her teeth. She was actually eager to put Melanie through the wringer.

Melanie was jumpy as a June bug. She'd been skittish ever since Mike had arrived with a load of topsoil first thing Monday morning. If he didn't know better, he'd actually think she was scared of him. What the hell had her sisters asked about him after he'd left on Saturday?

"Have a good visit with your sisters?" he asked, eyeing her curiously.

"Great."

"They go back home?"

"Last night," she confirmed.

"You sleep okay?"

She frowned at him. "I slept just fine. Why do you ask?"

"You look the way you did that first morning I showed up here, edgy and out of sorts. The only thing missing is the lamp."

She stared at him blankly.

He chuckled. "You're not clutching it so you can crack my skull open with it, but you do look as if you don't quite trust me."

"Oh."

"Don't want to talk about it," he concluded.

"About what?"

"Whatever has you so edgy."

"Not really."

"Okay." He dumped a wheelbarrow filled with rich topsoil in a cleared spot in the backyard, then headed back to his truck for more.

Melanie trailed after him, silent and clearly troubled. Eventually she sighed heavily.

Mike stopped shoveling dirt into the wheelbarrow and stared at her. "Okay, that's it. Something is obviously on your mind. Spill."

"It's nuts."

"Maybe so, but it's bugging you, so ask."

"My sisters think I should ask if you're still carrying the torch for your ex-wife," she said, color flooding her cheeks.

Mike's pulse throbbed dully. "Who actually wants to know? You or them?"

"All of us, I guess."

"No," he said succinctly, hoping that would put an end to it.

"Is Jessie your only child?"

He regarded her incredulously. Where the hell had they come up with that one? "Yes," he said tightly. "Did you think I kept two or three more stuffed in a closet somewhere? Or that I'd left them with a woman who's addicted to drugs?"

She flushed at that. "No, of course not. I just had to be sure."

He couldn't help wondering if this had something to do with whoever had sent her scurrying away from Boston. What the hell had that guy—and he was assuming a man was at the root of her flight—done to her?

He gave her a quizzical look. "Anything else?"

"And you have full custody of Jessie?"

"Yes."

"I see."

He glanced over at her. "What is it you think you see?"

"Nothing. I just meant… Oh, hell, I don't know what I meant."

"If you're out of questions and you're not going to help me spread this topsoil, go find something else to do," he suggested curtly. "Or at least drop the inquisition. Something tells me it has less to do with me than it does with that past you refuse to discuss."

A wounded expression in her eyes quickly turned to wariness. She whirled away and headed toward the house. "I'll be inside if you need me."

After she'd gone, Mike sighed. He'd made a mess of that. She'd only been asking perfectly reasonable questions. Well, except for that one about him having more kids. That one was out of left field. Still, it wasn't her fault that the whole subject of his marriage and divorce was so damn touchy. He thought he'd already made that clear to her, but obviously her sisters had filled her head with a lot of doubts and nonsense about him. He could hardly blame them for wanting to look out for her, especially when it was so plain that someone had hurt her recently, but that didn't make it any easier to be asked about all that stuff he preferred to block out of his mind.

Hell, *he* should have been the one asking questions. He should have pushed harder to find out who'd hurt her and how. Maybe then he'd know just how fragile Melanie was and whether he was destined to do the same thing to her.

The questions would have to wait for another day, though. Or at least until he worked off this ridiculous desire to go inside and kiss her senseless. If things between them were confusing now, that would pretty much send the complication meter into the stratosphere.

Melanie stood by the window and tried not to stare. Mike's shirt was stretched taut over flexing muscles as he shoveled the topsoil from his truck onto a growing mound in the area he'd designated for a perennial garden. She'd made an absolute mess of things just now. She knew what a private man he was, at least when it came to his marriage. Why on earth had she allowed her sisters to prod her into poking around in his personal business?

Of course, the answer was obvious. She wanted to know. She'd been burned all too recently by a man who'd kept silent about the important relationships in his life. She'd learned from bitter experience that she was incapable of telling when a man was lying to her.

Not that it mattered in Mike's case, of course. It wasn't like she was getting involved with him. Her emotions weren't on the line. Her future wasn't at stake. What did it really matter if he still had feelings for Jessie's mother?

She glanced outside, saw that he'd stripped off his shirt, and sighed. She was lying through her teeth. She wanted him, all right. Her sisters had seen that immediately. That's why they'd spent the entire weekend poking and prodding and asking all those unanswerable questions about Mike. They'd obviously seen her all but drooling over him. They'd definitely seen the way he kissed her. And they knew her well enough to understand that as clever and sneaky as Mike might be, that kiss would never have happened if Melanie hadn't wanted it to. She could duck an unwanted advance with the best of them.

She ought to go out there right now and apologize for poking into things that were none of her concern, but the truth was, she did need to know the answers to those questions. She did need to protect herself before this thing with Mike, whatever it was, went one step further.

Of course, he would only say he'd already answered her. Unfortunately, his curt, one-word replies had only stirred more questions.

It took a while, but she finally gathered her courage and went back outside. He glanced up, nodded, then went right on raking the topsoil over the ground.

"I'm sorry," she said.

He stopped then and leaned on the rake. "Really?"

She flinched under his steady, disbelieving gaze. "Okay, I'm not sorry for asking, only for making you uncomfortable."

"Thought so."

"They're reasonable questions, Mike."

"Yes," he agreed. "But I don't have any other answers."

"You could elaborate."

"Have you elaborated on why you came up here looking like a wounded soul?"

"It's not the same thing."

"Isn't it? How do you figure that?"

"What happened to me is over."

"My marriage is over."

"Not as long as you have Jessie," she pointed out. "Jessie ties you to her mother forever. Linda could be in rehab right now trying to get her act together to come back to you."

"I hope she is in rehab," Mike said. "But she won't be coming back to me. That door is closed."

He sounded so sure of that. Melanie wanted desperately to believe him. Some crazy part of her wanted to take a risk and get closer to him, even if it was only for a few short weeks. But despite the finite end to their relationship that was in the cards, there were far too many emotional perils to be weighed.

He stepped across the freshly raked dirt and stood directly in front of her, tipping her chin up until she couldn't avoid his gaze.

"Linda is not an issue," he repeated softly. "This is between you and me."

Before she could question his declaration, before she could say that old baggage couldn't simply be dismissed, his mouth covered hers and her senses went haywire, just as they had on the previous occasions when they'd kissed.

She couldn't think, couldn't remember even one of the questions she'd meant to ask. All she could do was feel the way his lips caressed hers, the way his heat and scent surrounded her, the way his body fit hers, the play of his muscles under her fingers when her hands drifted to his sun-warmed shoulders to cling to him.

It seemed like an eternity passed—or maybe only a split second—before he released her and went back to raking as if nothing the least bit monumental or life-altering had just occurred.

How the heck could he be so cool not ten seconds after sending her up in flames? she wondered irritably.

If she hadn't already had her sisters' warnings screaming in her head, that kiss would have been a wake-up call. She was up to her eyebrows, not in topsoil but in quicksand…and she was sinking fast.

Chapter Eight

He had to stop kissing her, Mike thought as he concentrated on getting that topsoil spread out just so, mainly to avoid meeting Melanie's eyes. She was watching him warily. He could almost feel her gaze boring into him. He could practically hear the endless list of questions on the tip of her tongue.

Like what the hell was he thinking? He didn't have an answer to that one.

Or what did he want from her? He didn't have an answer to that one, either, at least not one that wouldn't get him slapped silly. Oh, yes, he wanted to haul her into bed, but that was not exactly what she was itching to hear right now. And since he wasn't going to let it happen, anyway, it was a moot point.

There were probably a whole litany of questions he hadn't even thought of. Heck, there were probably a few that hadn't even occurred to her sisters, and they were the grand masters of asking the unanswerable.

"We need to talk," she finally said, sounding as edgy as she had when he'd first arrived.

His gaze narrowed. The very last thing on his mind was talking. What was it with women that they wanted to talk about everything? The only woman in his life who'd ever kept silent was Linda, only because she'd had so blasted many secrets she wanted to keep from him.

"About?" he asked cautiously.

"I can't talk to you when you're only half-dre…" She blushed furiously. "When half your attention is on that dirt. Put on your shirt and come inside. I just made some iced tea."

Inside? Mike stared at her. Inside was a very bad idea. Inside was where her bed was. Inside was where no casual passerby could happen to see whatever they were up to. Inside was damned dangerous.

"I'm filthy," he protested, grabbing at the most obvious and convenient straw. "Why don't you bring the tea out here? We can sit on the swing." The chance of a passing boater intruding on their privacy was slim, but it might be enough to keep his hands where they belonged…away from her.

"I'm not worried about you tracking a little dirt through the house," she said impatiently. "Besides, it's hot out here. I've turned on the air-conditioning. The kitchen will be cool."

Not as cool as the ice-cold shower he needed at the moment, Mike thought desperately. "Give me a minute," he said, hoping to buy himself enough time to talk himself out of the insane desire he had to just go with the flow and haul her straight upstairs to her bed. "Go on in. I'll be there."

She regarded him skeptically, as if she didn't entirely trust him not to take off, which, come to think of it, wasn't a bad idea. Cowardly, but not a bad idea under the circumstances.

"Go," he repeated. "I won't be long."

She nodded and walked toward the house, her hips swaying provocatively in what was more than likely a totally instinctive and unintended turn-on. He was such a jerk. Women walked past him all the time with the deliberate intention of trying to snag his attention. Brenda put more sway into her caboose when she sashayed past his table at the café than any woman he'd ever seen. It never did a thing for him. Melanie walked away, all innocence and hurt feelings, and he wanted to jump her bones. Ridiculous. He really had been celibate way too long.

He yanked on his shirt and buttoned it all the way to his neck as if that might prevent her from getting any wild ideas about dragging it right back off him. Then he spent another ten minutes getting his hormones and his wayward thoughts under control before he followed.

En route to the house, he gave himself a very stern lecture on what was *not* going to happen. Whatever Melanie's agenda, he was going to sit across from her at the kitchen table and keep his damn hands to himself. He was going to listen politely, nod when it was called for, then hightail it out of there at the first opportunity.

Inside, he found her pacing. She frowned at him as if he were unexpected and as if he'd caught her doing something vaguely compromising.

"Sit down," she said at last.

She took her own place at the table. Ignoring the full

glass of iced tea in front of her, she folded her hands primly on top of the scarred table, her expression troubled. His tea was waiting for him in front of the seat next to her.

Mike snagged the glass and moved to the opposite end of the table, grateful that it was one of those oval things with a leaf inserted. That ought to be sufficient distance to keep him on his best behavior.

Her brow rose at his actions, but she didn't comment. Instead, she met his gaze and asked, "What are we going to do about this?"

Mike tried to pretend he didn't have a clue what she meant. "This?"

"Us. The kissing."

Curiosity and that flustered expression on her face got the better of him. "What do you want to do about it?"

"It needs to stop," she said at once.

"Which isn't exactly an answer to the question I asked, is it? Do you want it to stop?"

Temper flashed in her eyes. "What am I supposed to say to that? If I say yes, you'll call me a liar, since it's obvious I'm as much into it as you are. If I say no, then I'm opening myself up to something I don't want to happen."

He gave her a quizzical look. "In other words, the kissing is okay, but what you really want to stop is anything more? Am I interpreting what you said accurately?" He really needed to be very clear, because one tiny miscue and they'd both wind up in bed…in flames.

"Why are you making this so difficult?" she asked with a trace of annoyance. "We're adults. We should be able to decide in a perfectly rational way to quit playing dangerous games. We both know this can't go anywhere.

You have your reasons. I have mine. They're all valid. Let's stop tempting fate."

Mike couldn't help it, he had to ask. He was a man, after all. "Then you are tempted?"

"Oh, don't be an idiot," she snapped. "You know I am, or we wouldn't be having this conversation."

"What would we be doing?" Mike asked. He was fascinated with the way her mind worked. She'd obviously given this a lot of thought since coming inside. He wondered if her thoughts had paralleled his own. He wondered if she was having half as much difficulty as he was listening to her head, rather than her hormones.

"I'd have slapped you out there and put an end to any more wild ideas about you kissing me," she insisted, though not very forcefully. She didn't sound as if she believed it for a minute.

"So, instead you're going to talk it to death," he concluded. "Maybe get a written agreement, spelling out the parameters for all future contact?"

She sighed, her cheeks flushed. "When you say it like that, it sounds absurd."

"It *is* absurd. I think we can control ourselves. I think we can prevent anything from happening that we don't want to have happen."

"In a perfect world, yes, we could," she agreed.

Mike finally caught on to what was really worrying her. "But you're just a little bit afraid that this isn't a perfect world," he suggested. "You're worried that one of these days one of us will snap and lose our heads, and all these good intentions will go flying out the window."

"Exactly."

"That could happen even if we put the rules in writing

and have them notarized," he informed her. "You know what they say about the road to hell."

"Yeah, that it's paved with good intentions. Okay, bottom line, I don't want this to get any more complicated than it already is." She leveled a look straight into his eyes. "I'm trusting you to see that it doesn't."

Mike stared at her. Well, hell. His intentions were every bit as solid as hers, but that didn't mean he was a saint. "You probably shouldn't do that."

"Well, I do," she insisted, looking pleased with herself. "Let's get back to work."

She was up and out the door before Mike could gather his composure, much less his thoughts. The naive woman had just dumped all responsibility for whatever happened between them from here on out on his shoulders. She'd planted a virtual No Trespassing sign in front of her and expected him to honor it. If she'd wanted to fill his head with nonstop schemes for getting around such a thing, she couldn't have done a more effective job. Getting her into bed was just about the only thought dancing around in his brain. It was crowding out all the sane, rational reasons for keeping his distance. It was nudging aside all of *his* rules for keeping his life uncomplicated.

Oh, he was going to sleep with her. No question about it.

And then he was going to hate himself for letting it happen.

Melanie was rather proud of herself. For once she'd taken the initiative, laid all her cards on the table and told a man exactly what she wanted—or in this case, what she didn't want. Mike had seemed a little startled by her honesty, but in the end he was bound to admire a woman who knew her own mind. And of course he was bound to be grateful that she'd set ground rules that would keep things from getting complicated for either one of them.

Of course, that analysis didn't explain why he was watching her as warily as someone keeping a close eye on a snake that was coiled to strike. In fact, he seemed downright edgy, when the exact opposite should have been the case. He should be relieved.

"Is something wrong?" she asked eventually, poised at the edge of the pile of topsoil, rake in hand.

"Nothing," he said grimly.

"Then why do you keep looking at me like that?"

"Like what?"

"As if I'm some strange species you've never encountered before."

He chuckled. "You're a female. That's strange enough. Men far wiser than I have spent entire lifetimes trying to figure you out."

"There's no need to be insulting."

"Actually I find the way your mind works rather intriguing."

"Oh? In what way?"

He shook his head. "You really don't have a clue, do you?"

"About what?"

"That now that you've declared yourself off-limits, all I can think about is how to get around that."

She swallowed hard and stared at him. That was definitely not what she'd intended. Or was it? "Are you serious?"

"Very."

"But we just agreed—"

"Not exactly, darlin'. You reached a conclusion, put

me in charge of following the rules, than sashayed away as if there was nothing more to worry about.''

"Because I trust you."

"You shouldn't. I told you that inside."

"But you don't want to get involved with someone who's leaving town soon, do you?"

"No."

"And I don't want to get mixed up in something that could get complicated and messy."

"So you say."

"Do you doubt me?"

"Intellectually, I think you believe that."

"I *do* believe it," she said emphatically.

"Then you obviously have no idea how men's minds work. Tell us to stay away and all we want is the opposite."

She regarded him incredulously. "But that's just perverse," she said.

"True, but it's a fact of life."

"So now you want to have sex, even though we both know it's a terrible idea?"

He grinned. "Pretty much."

"It's not going to happen," she declared.

His grin spread. "Is that a challenge? Oh, boy, now you're really making it interesting."

Melanie stared at him, trying to fight the sudden desire to take her rake to him. "You're just tormenting me," she accused, aware that now the idea of sex was firmly planted in her head, too. "You're getting some kind of kick out of watching me squirm."

"I think you've got that backward. You're the one doing the tormenting. This is verbal foreplay, darlin'."

Shocked that he could have leaped to such a conclusion, she snapped, "Don't you foreplay me, Mr. Mikelewski. Right this second I wouldn't get anywhere near you if you were the last man on the planet.''

He laughed. ''Uh-oh, now you've done it. You've questioned my ability to change your mind.'' He took a step toward her. ''Want me to see how quickly I can prove you wrong?''

Melanie backed up, her pulse humming with something that felt a lot more like anticipation than anxiety. Was this the outcome she'd subconsciously been after? Surely not.

''No, I most certainly do not.'' Liar, liar, liar. The voice in her head was raising quite a din.

His gaze never left her face. ''You sure?''

''Very sure,'' she declared, though some traitorous part of her was all but shouting that the opposite was true.

Mike laid down his rake, his expression suddenly sober. ''Think about it, Melanie. Because the next time I come by, we won't just be talking about this. We'll be testing all those rules of yours.''

When he walked right on past her without so much as a casual touch, she stood there trembling, maybe with outrage, more likely with need. Damn, he was right. All this talk had obviously made both of them want the exact opposite of what they knew was sensible.

''You're spending a lot of time at the Lindsey cottage lately,'' Jeff observed when he and Mike took a break on a job a few days later.

Since Mike was still wrestling with his conscience over the game he and Melanie were playing, he was in no mood to get drawn into this particular discussion with his best friend. Jeff tended to cut through the crap, and Mike was trying very hard not to be totally honest with himself. He feared if he admitted the truth, he'd be over at that cottage like a shot.

"The garden's almost finished," he said tersely.

"As if you being there has anything to do with the garden," Jeff commented dryly.

"That is my *only* reason for being there," Mike insisted.

"Maybe it started out that way, but something tells me things have changed. What would be so wrong about you getting together with Melanie D'Angelo?"

"If she were the type to have a casual fling, nothing. But she's not."

"Then have a serious fling with her," Jeff said reasonably. "You're long overdue for one. You're single. She's single. Maybe it'll develop into something amazing."

"I can't take that chance," Mike replied. "I have a daughter to consider, and Melanie's made it clear she's going back to Boston."

"Change her mind. I notice she hasn't left yet. Something around here must be interesting enough to keep her right where she is."

"She's on an extended vacation, that's all."

"People fall in love with this area all the time. Her grandmother did. You did. Maybe she will. Give her a reason to stay."

"Maybe's not good enough, not for Jessie," Mike said, sticking to his guns. "She wants a mom. I don't want her to get attached to Melanie and have that rug yanked out from under her."

"I suppose you have a point," Jeff conceded. "You do have to consider Jessie." He gave Mike a sideways glance. "Seems a shame, though. I haven't seen you this happy since you moved here."

"Maybe I'm happy because you actually turned up today with some decent-looking plants," Mike teased, hoping to divert Jeff's attention.

"And maybe pigs fly," Jeff retorted. "My plants are always excellent, and you know it. Your good mood doesn't have a damn thing to do with me. It's all tied up with that woman you claim you're not the least bit interested in."

"I never said I wasn't interested," Mike grumbled. "Only that it's not going to go anywhere."

"Seems like a waste not to give it a chance," Jeff repeated. "Pam says—"

"Heaven protect me from whatever your wife has to say about my love life."

"She says you're just scared," Jeff continued doggedly. "I can't blame you, but you're letting life pass you by."

Mike sighed heavily. "Yeah, it seems that way to me, too."

He didn't realize he'd muttered the wistful words aloud until he heard Jeff's hoot and saw the grin spreading across his face.

"Told you so," Jeff gloated.

"Go to hell."

"No way, pal. I'm sticking around to watch this one play itself out. It's the most entertainment I've had in years."

"Then you must be leading a very dull life."

"Not half as dull as yours before you met Melanie," Jeff reminded him. "Something you ought to consider when Jessie's in bed tonight and you're staring at the TV with nothing but a beer for company."

Unfortunately, Mike had spent several nights just like that lately. Jeff was right. His life was boring. Melanie

D'Angelo could change that. He just had to figure out if it was worth the risk.

He thought of the way she'd felt when she was in his arms, of the need that thundered through him. It was pretty damn irresistible, all right.

If only he understood what was holding Melanie back, if only she would open up to him about her past, maybe then he'd know if the pleasures outweighed the risks. Until that time, he needed to proceed with caution.

Chapter Nine

Melanie stared at the tuna on rye on her plate, trying to figure out how anyone could manage to screw up such a basic sandwich. It had so much mayo and sweet relish in it, it was virtually impossible to taste the tuna. She couldn't help but wonder if this was yet another of Brenda's attempts to discourage her from coming into the café, or even from staying in town.

She was trying to work up some enthusiasm for finishing the tasteless sandwich when an unfamiliar man slid into the booth opposite her.

"Hey," he said with an engaging grin. "You're Melanie D'Angelo, right?"

She was still getting used to the fact that no one in this small town thought twice about approaching a stranger. If this man hadn't been wearing a wedding ring in plain sight, she would have worried he was hitting on her, but there was nothing but simple friendliness in his demeanor. She nodded.

"Thought so. I'm Jeff Clayborne, a friend of Mike's. I've heard a lot about you."

Clayborne? That was the name of the nursery they'd gone to. And this was Mike's friend. She couldn't help wondering how Mike had explained their relationship.

"Oh? What exactly does Mike say about me?" she said just to see what sort of response it would elicit.

He grinned, evidently responding to the edginess she hadn't been able to disguise. "No need to panic. It's all been good. That's why it's been so intriguing."

She wasn't sure what to say to that.

Jeff wasn't the least bit put off by her silence. He gave her an intense look. "So, I was wondering if you'd like to come to dinner at our house one night. My wife's dying to meet you."

She stared at him blankly. "Why?"

"Because you're the first woman Mike's ever shown the slightest interest in," he said candidly.

"So she wants to check me out," Melanie concluded. "Why don't you just tell her she has nothing to worry about. Nothing's going on between Mike and me."

Jeff regarded her with barely suppressed amusement.

Melanie frowned at his blatantly skeptical reaction. "Why is that funny?"

"Because you're both in denial."

"I'm not denying anything," Melanie responded half-heartedly. "Mike took an interest in my grandmother's garden. That's it."

"Really?" Jeff said, still not bothering to hide his skepticism.

"Yes, really," she replied.

"Mike's been driving past that house every day since

he moved to town. If he was so fascinated by the garden, why didn't he do something about it before?'' Jeff challenged.

"Oh, I don't know. Maybe he has a thing about trespassing,'' she suggested sarcastically.

He laughed again. "That's one possibility. Personally, I think my explanation makes more sense.''

A shadow fell over the table. "What explanation is that?'' Mike inquired, his voice chilly.

Melanie's gaze snapped up to meet his. She glanced toward Jeff. She noticed that there wasn't the slightest hint of guilt in his expression at having been caught meddling in his friend's personal life.

Mike slid into the booth next to her and scowled at Jeff. "Well?''

"I was just inviting Melanie to dinner at the house one night,'' Jeff said easily, ignoring Mike's question.

"Really? Did she accept?''

"Nope. As a matter of fact, she turned me down.''

Mike nodded approvingly. "Smart woman.''

"Well, I guess I'll leave you two alone,'' Jeff said. He winked at Melanie. "If you change your mind about dinner—or about anything else—let us know.''

"I won't change my mind,'' Melanie said with less confidence than she might have if Mike's thigh hadn't been pressed to hers. It was just about all she could think about.

When Jeff was gone, Mike scooted away from her as if the contact was too much for him, too. "I'm sorry if he made you uncomfortable. He and Pam have become good friends since I moved here. They think that gives them the right to poke around in my personal life.''

"It was no big deal,'' she said.

He studied her intently. "You sure about that?''

"Absolutely."

"Okay, then. How've you been?"

"Fine. You?"

"Fine."

They fell into an awkward silence. Melanie desperately wanted to break it but couldn't think of a single thing to say. The only thing she really wanted to know was where he'd been and why he hadn't come by the house for days. She already knew the answer, though. Mike was avoiding her. She could hardly blame him.

"Sorry I haven't been by lately," he said as if he'd read her mind. "I've had a big job to complete before the owners get down here next week. They want the landscaping finished before their housewarming party."

Something that felt a lot like relief washed over her. "Will you make it?"

"If Jeff stops meddling in my personal life and gets all the plants over there," Mike said.

"I suppose he meant well."

"The same way your sisters meant well," he replied. He met her gaze and held it for what seemed like an eternity. He seemed to be debating with himself about something. "Do you want to go out with me?" he asked eventually.

She swallowed hard under the intensity of his gaze. "On a date?"

"Call it whatever you want to." He shrugged. "It's just dinner."

"I don't know." She managed to get the lukewarm response out, even though her libido was screaming an emphatic *yes*.

"It wouldn't have to be a big deal. And it definitely wouldn't involve Jeff and Pam putting us under a microscope to dissect our every move."

But it would be a big deal, whether Jeff and Pam were there or not, she thought desperately. It would be a very big deal. Because if she went out with Mike, if he so much as touched her, there would be no turning back.

Mike wasn't sure what had possessed him to ask Melanie out, not after everything they'd both done to see that their hormones didn't get the best of them. Maybe it was the vulnerability he'd seen in her eyes when he'd offered an explanation for why he'd stayed away. He'd realized then that his absence had actually mattered to her. He'd suddenly wanted to prove that he hadn't been avoiding her, that he wasn't some macho jerk who teased a woman, planted all sorts of ideas in her head, then never followed through.

Maybe he also wanted to prove the same thing to himself. Maybe he wanted to make a liar out of Jeff with his smug declaration that Mike was in denial about his feelings.

Maybe he just wanted another chance to kiss Melanie and make mincemeat out of all those rules she'd established. That was probably the one, he admitted to himself. He'd thought about little else since the last time he'd set eyes on her. All those rules and challenges were practically irresistible.

"Tonight," he pressed when Melanie had been silent way too long. "Jessie can spend a couple of extra hours with the sitter." He liked that. Knowing that Jessie couldn't be left with anyone for too long would keep the evening short. There would be no danger of anything getting out of hand. Yep, that was a great plan.

Melanie nodded slowly, as if she got the implied message. There would be no hanky-panky, no dangerous lingering under the stars, lips locked, hands roaming.

"Okay, then," she said at last. "Just dinner."

Mike bit back a smile. She sounded so emphatic. "I'll pick you up at six."

"And have me home by eight," she added.

"Or thereabouts," he agreed. After all, even he wasn't delusional enough not to leave himself *some* wiggle room. Just in case, he'd leave things a little loose with the sitter.

He glanced into Melanie's eyes and felt his pulse scramble.

Maybe, just in case, he'd see if the sitter could spend the night.

Dinner was lovely. It was a starlit night, and they were able to sit on the restaurant's deck and linger over coffee.

True to his word, Mike had Melanie back at the cottage by eight, but then he suggested a stroll down to the river. She couldn't seem to deny herself that much.

The moon shimmered on the surface of the water. A soft breeze stirred the balmy air.

"It's beautiful," Melanie murmured, caught up in the tranquility of the night.

"Beautiful," Mike echoed, his voice sounding oddly choked.

Melanie turned and saw that his gaze was on her. Her own breath caught in her throat.

"Mike," she whispered.

"Don't talk," he said, leaning down until his mouth hovered over hers. "Don't say another word."

And then he apparently forgot all about the rules and kissed her as if there was no tomorrow. Melanie thought she was going to go up in flames just from the simple touch of his lips on hers. It was as if she'd been waiting her whole life for this man. Doubts fled as passion stirred.

"I want you so much," Mike whispered, his breath ragged. "I know it's a lousy idea. I know we swore we weren't going to let this happen, but I'm not sure I can go another minute without making love to you." His gaze searched hers. "How do you feel about that? Say the word and we'll pretend this never happened."

Pretend it had never happened? That would be next to impossible, Melanie thought as her blood hummed. The memory of his mouth on hers, of his hands skimming over her breasts, was forever seared on her brain. She'd known what it was like to want a man, but not to crave him, not like this. There was no way in hell she could go back fifteen minutes and pretend nothing had ever happened.

"Don't stop," she whispered at last. "Please don't stop."

He scooped her into his arms, and before she knew it, they were in her room, in her bed, and nothing else mattered. Not her own lousy choices in the past, not whatever secrets Mike might still be keeping from her. All that mattered were his tenderness and undisguised need for her.

It scared her how much she'd come to need Mike in such a brief time, but she had no idea how to fight the feelings. They simply were.

Someday she would need answers, but not tonight. Tonight all she needed was Mike.

His rough hands were gentle on her skin, the callused fingers wickedly clever as they manipulated the delicate buttons on her blouse until it fell away, exposing her lacy bra and bare flesh. His eyes turned dark with passion as he took his time surveying her before a deft flick of his fingers had her bra undone and she was entirely naked from the waist up.

His mouth captured the tip of her breast, his tongue circling the nipple until it was a tight, hard bud capable of sending shock waves straight to her toes.

He groaned and fell back on the bed. ''It's been too long. I'm never going to last unless we slow things down.''

Melanie reached for the hem of his T-shirt, sliding her fingers along the hard flesh of his abdomen before she lifted the shirt free of his jeans, then tugged it over his head. ''I don't want to go slow,'' she said. ''I want everything now.''

He grinned. ''Impatient, huh?''

''Maybe it's a female thing. Once we know what we want, we don't like waiting for it.''

He cupped her cheeks. ''And you know what you want where I'm concerned?''

''I want this,'' she said at once.

''And nothing more?'' he asked, his expression solemn. ''There can't be anything more.''

''I know that,'' she said. ''I'm leaving, anyway. All any of us has is the here and now.''

He regarded her skeptically. ''That's very philosophical, but is it the way you really feel?''

Melanie sat back, vaguely irritated by the string of questions. ''Do you think I don't know my own mind?''

''No, of course not, but I saw the way you were with your family. I know closeness must be what you want for yourself, and I can't be anything more than an interlude.''

''You don't have the right to assume you know what I want out of life,'' she retorted, realizing even as she spoke that the argument was rapidly escalating out of control.

"Then tell me what you want."

The request deflated her anger. Instead, an exasperated laugh escaped. "You want to have that conversation *now?*"

He tucked his hands behind his head and leaned back against the pillows, looking relaxed and sexy as sin. "Yes, I think I do."

"Are you crazy?"

He laughed. "More than likely. Heaven knows, I'll probably be convinced of that in the morning." He winked. "Then again, maybe you can convince me that you really do want a fling and we'll both leave this bed satisfied."

"You're impossible." She studied his expression. "But you're not giving in on this, are you?"

"No."

"What about getting home early?"

"Jessie's fine. Tell me what you want, Melanie."

She sighed heavily and fell back against the pillows next to him. "I wanted to make love to you. I wanted to know what it would be like to have you inside me, filling me up, making me scream."

Mike swallowed hard next to her. Good. He deserved to be squirming about now.

"And long-term?" he asked, his voice ragged. "What do you want for the long haul?"

"I have no idea," she said honestly. "I've been trying very hard lately not to think too far into the future. I've been discovering that there are advantages to living in the moment, to not having too many unrealistic expectations."

Frustrated as she was, she found herself glancing at him. "What about you? What do you want long-term?"

"To make a decent home for my daughter," he said without hesitation. "To do work I enjoy."

"What about having someone to share it with?" she asked, voicing the one longing she hadn't been able to push out of her own heart no matter how hard she'd tried.

"An unrealistic expectation," he said tightly.

"Because you won't let yourself trust another woman?"

He nodded. "I can't. If it were only me, maybe I could take that chance, but I won't put Jessie through losing someone else, just because I'd like to have someone to come home to at night."

She propped herself up on her elbow and leveled a look straight into his eyes. "You know what I think? I think it doesn't have anything at all to do with Jessie. I think you're scared of getting your heart broken again. I think you're the one who hasn't recovered from not being important enough to your ex-wife for her to do anything necessary to get off the drugs and save your marriage."

Mike's gaze never wavered. He never even flinched under the harsh accusation.

"You're probably right," he said at last. "If I hold on to the anger, if I remember every minute of the day and night what it was like to watch Linda self-destruct and abandon Jessie and me, even when she was still right there in the same room, then I won't ever make that mistake again."

"That's sad," Melanie said.

"Are you any better?" he challenged her. "Are you

ready to plunge right in and take another chance on love?''

''I'm here, aren't I?''

''Sure,'' he agreed. ''Because I'm a safe bet. I've made it plain I'm not looking for anything more than right here and right now and, for tonight, anyway, that suits you. You're as much of a coward as I am, Melanie.'' He gave her a sad look. ''Worse, you won't even talk about why.''

She shivered as the truth hit home. ''Because I'm ashamed of what happened,'' she suddenly told him. ''The man I was involved with, the man I thought I knew so well, the man I loved, turned out to be married with two kids.''

Mike stared at her incredulously. ''Turned out to be? You didn't know?''

''I had no idea,'' she admitted. ''There were probably a million signs, but I either didn't recognize them or ignored them because I didn't want to know the truth. So now you know. I'm an idiot.''

He touched her cheek. ''You trusted him and he lied to you. *He's* the idiot.''

''At least now you know why my sisters were so determined to ask all those questions when they found out about you. They didn't trust me to get it right this time, either.''

''I've been honest with you from the beginning,'' he said. ''I might not elaborate too much, but I've told you the basics.''

''So, what now?'' she asked. ''Are we just using each other for sex?''

''Nobody's using anybody,'' Mike said fiercely. ''We're just clearing up the ground rules, deciding if we want to go on.''

"If we have to think this much, maybe it's the wrong thing to do," she admitted reluctantly, then moaned. "I can't believe I'm in bed, half-naked with a gorgeous man, and suggesting that we call the whole thing off."

"Frankly, that goes double for me." He glanced sideways at her. "Now that everything's crystal clear, we could pick up where we left off."

Melanie poked him in the ribs. "Not a chance. Honesty has thoroughly spoiled the mood."

He leaned over her, his mouth just above hers. "Bet we could recapture it in a heartbeat."

Her heart skipped a beat, and renewed heat spread through her. "Think so?"

"I know so," he said, right before he claimed her mouth and kissed her until she was writhing beneath him.

"Hmm," she murmured, when she finally caught her breath. "I guess I was wrong."

"Wrong about what?"

"Honesty's one heck of a turn-on, after all." She had no idea why she'd waited so long to tell Mike the truth. Now there were no secrets left to bite either of them in the butt.

When morning came, Mike rolled out of bed, grabbed his pants and headed for the shower. He hadn't felt this alive in a long, long time. There was something about energetic sex that set the blood to humming in a way that nothing else on earth could do.

When he emerged from the bathroom, Melanie was sprawled across the whole bed, the sheet twisted around her in a way that revealed far more than it concealed. His body responded at once, and his plan to get to work

early and pretend this was just an ordinary day promptly
fell by the wayside.

He sat down on the edge of the bed and smoothed his
hand over her rounded backside. The little whimpering
sound that emerged from low in her throat reminded him
of all the other sexy little moans she'd uttered when
they'd made love.

"Wake up, darlin'," he murmured, pressing a kiss to
the hollow at the base of her spine.

"Is it morning?" she asked sleepily.

"It is by my standards."

"You leaving?"

"That was the plan," he said.

She rolled over and squinted at him. "Was?" she echoed, sounding intrigued by the possibilities.

"Unless you're interested in having me stay," he said.

"For breakfast?" she taunted.

"Maybe later."

"Ah." She reached up and touched the damp curls
on his chest. "You've already taken a shower."

"True."

"And you're half-dressed."

"Only half," he emphasized.

"So it wouldn't take much to persuade you to get
undressed?" she concluded, clearly amused.

"Not much at all," he agreed. "Maybe a kiss."

"I can do that," she said, reaching for him and giving
him a chaste peck on the cheek.

Mike laughed. "You'll have to do better than that.
Think you're up to it?"

She wound her fingers through his hair and kissed him
thoroughly until there was no question at all of leaving.
The only question was how fast he could get out of his
jeans and back inside her.

She was ready for him, her hips arching to meet him, her body already straining toward yet another hard, fast climax that sent shudders sweeping through her right before they triggered his own explosion.

Sweet heaven, he thought, collapsing. How had he missed the fact that urgent, demanding sex could be just as rewarding as long, lingering caresses and a slow buildup of anticipation? The night had been filled with the full range of experiences, each one more satisfying than the one before.

And still it hadn't been enough. He would want Melanie again in an hour or a day or a month. The realization slammed into him like a freight train. Panic followed, clawing at him, churning up a fight-or-flight reaction that made him want to leap from the bed and head for the door. Only an awareness that Melanie didn't deserve that kind of cowardly escape kept him where he was, silent and withdrawn, but at least present. She'd trusted him with her deepest secret last night, told him about the man who'd lied to her and betrayed her. He couldn't prove that he was just as much of a lowlife in his own way by running out on her now.

Next to him she sighed. "You can go," she said softly. "I know you want to."

"No, I…" he began, but the protest died in his throat when he saw the knowing amusement lurking in the depths of her eyes.

"It's okay, really. Go pick up Jessie. I'll be fine. No expectations, Mike. That was our agreement."

"It doesn't feel right to take off on you like that," he said.

"I'm not responsible for your conscience," she told him. "You do have my permission to go, though."

Because he did need to pick up Jessie and get her to

school, because he was terrified of what he was feeling for Melanie right this instant, he crawled from the bed and pulled on his clothes.

"I'll call you later or stop by," he said, looking down at her. "Maybe the three of us can do something tonight."

Melanie shook her head. "Not tonight."

"Why? Do you have other plans?"

"No. I just think we both need to take a step back and remember what we talked about here last night, not just how it felt to be together. The sex was fabulous, but the words were just as important, Mike. We can't let ourselves forget them, not for a minute."

Mike bit back a sigh. She was right. "I will call you later today, though."

Her smile didn't quite reach her eyes. "That would be nice."

He turned and left the room, her words echoing in his ears. *Nice.* Wasn't that just *special,* he thought derisively. They were reducing something incredible to nothing, minimizing it so they could both live with it. What the hell were they thinking?

Chapter Ten

There was a wicked gleam in Pam's eye when she cornered Mike in the supermarket. Since he was well aware that Jeff's wife had a tendency to meddle, it was worrisome. So far he'd evaded all of her clever machinations to fix him up, but there was always a first time for her to sneak in under his radar with one of her perfect-for-you dates.

"Well, hello there," Pam greeted him. "You're just the man I've been looking for."

Mike regarded her with amusement. "You must not have been looking too hard. I've been around, mostly with your husband. You do still keep track of him, don't you?"

She made a face. "Unfortunately, Jeff has forbidden me to come by the job sites."

Mike quirked an eyebrow. "He forbade you? That must have gone over well."

"He said I distract him. That made up for it." She shrugged. "Besides, I let him give orders from time to time, when it's not worth arguing over. It's good for the marriage."

Mike grinned. "I'll keep that little pearl of wisdom in mind, should the occasion ever arise."

"You should. It's very sound advice. Now, let's talk about when you're going to bring Melanie to dinner. I know Jeff invited her."

He should have guessed Pam was behind that invitation, even though Jeff had given the impression it was his own idea. In fact, since Jeff's wife had seen him with Melanie weeks ago at the nursery, he was a little surprised it had taken her so long.

"And she said no," he told her flatly. "I think we'll leave it like that."

"Why?"

"Because you'll make too much of it."

"I promise I'll be on my best behavior."

Mike chuckled. "Darlin', I've seen your best behavior. You could give Mike Wallace a run for his money when it comes to asking tough questions."

"Do the two of you have something to hide?" she inquired, her expression innocent.

"Nothing," Mike assured her.

"Then I don't see the problem. Besides, if you want Melanie to stay here, she needs to make friends. Jeff and I are eager to do our part to make her feel welcome, so she won't be quite so anxious to get back to Boston. She is still planning to go back, isn't she?" Pam asked sweetly. "How does that make you feel?"

Obviously she'd done her homework. Mike wondered how much information Jeff had passed on to his wife and how much she'd gleaned on her own. Pam had sources all over town.

"I am not having this conversation with you," he said tightly.

"I just want to help."

"How gracious and utterly unselfish of you," he said dryly.

She gave him a bland look. "We're your friends. It's the least we can do," she said magnanimously.

"I'm still not bringing Melanie over."

"How about if I invite her? Will you come, too?"

Mike saw the trap for what it was. "If she says yes, you bet I'll be there, but only to make sure you don't pester her to death."

Pam grinned, a satisfied glint in her eyes. "I'll call you with the details."

"She won't say yes."

She gave him a pitying look. "Wanna bet?"

"Twenty bucks."

"And you throw in the steaks," she challenged. "Thick New York strip steaks for four."

"Deal."

Mike stood there as Pam walked away, her expression triumphant. What had he been thinking? He knew precisely how sneaky and persuasive Pam could be. He might as well buy the blasted steaks now.

"Do you know some pint-size steamroller named Pam?" Melanie asked when Mike called that evening. She was still reeling from her encounter with the stranger who'd appeared on her doorstep earlier and wouldn't take no for an answer. While Jeff Clayborne had been friendly and persistent, his wife had taken persistence to an art form.

Mike groaned. "I was just calling to warn you she might call."

"Well, she didn't call. She came by."

"And?"

"We're having dinner there tomorrow night."

"How did that happen? I thought you were made of sterner stuff."

"Apparently," she said, her tone wry. "I heard about the bet. That pretty much clinched it."

"You wanted her to win?" he asked incredulously.

"No, I wanted to get to know the woman who could get you to agree to something so ridiculous. I think she might have some maneuvers I should know about."

"You don't really have to go," he told her.

Melanie laughed at the hopeful note in his voice. "Nice try, but it's too late. We're going. Jessie's invited, too, by the way."

"Pam doesn't miss a trick, does she?" he muttered.

"You should have known that. She's your friend, after all."

"I might have to reconsider that. What time?"

"Six. She said with the kids there, it would be better to make it an early night."

"I'll pick you up at quarter to six," he said, sounding resigned.

"*You* could stay home," Melanie said. "I actually only committed for myself. It's up to you if you want to honor your bet."

"Fat chance," Mike responded.

She laughed. "That's what Pam said you'd say."

"Damn straight. I'm not leaving you alone with that woman for a minute. If she's going to pry all your deep, dark secrets out of you, I want to be there."

For the first time since she'd agreed to dinner, Melanie

had serious second thoughts. She hadn't been considering Pam's actual mission when she'd caved in under pressure and accepted the woman's invitation. She'd merely been curious to see the interaction between Mike and this woman who seemed to know him so well. Besides, once again, days had passed since he'd been by to see her. To her regret, she'd missed him. Seeing him with other people around seemed like a safe way to satisfy her longing for a glimpse of him.

"You, Jessie and I could go out for pizza instead," she said wistfully. "In fact, I've been craving pizza for days now. One of those great big ones with everything on it."

"Sounds great, but I'm not sure you're prepared to have Pam hunt us down," Mike replied. "It wouldn't be pretty. Buck up, Melanie. I'm sure she'll make the inquisition as painless as possible."

"Maybe Jessie will be having a bad day tomorrow," Melanie suggested, only partially in jest.

"You would use a little girl to wriggle off the hook?" he asked, feigning shock.

"Yes," she answered without hesitation. "Yes, I would." And she wouldn't suffer a moment's guilty conscience.

"So would I," he admitted. "But my daughter loves going over there. Being around the Claybornes' daughter, Lyssa, is good for Jessie. I won't deny her that because the two of us are cowards."

Melanie heaved a resigned sigh. "Okay, then, I'll see you at five forty-five."

She was about to hang up when Mike said, "Hey, Melanie, one more thing you should probably keep in mind."

"What?"

"No touching. No kissing."

She laughed. That was a given, especially if they intended to at least maintain the illusion in public that there was absolutely nothing between them. "I don't think that will be a problem."

"Wanna bet?"

She sobered at once at the mischievous tone in his voice. "I think you've done enough betting for one day, Mike, don't you? How's that working for you?"

How had he let himself get drawn into spending an entire evening with Melanie under the watchful gaze of his two best friends? Mike wondered. All too recently he'd crawled out of her bed and vowed once more to steer clear of her entirely because the complications were getting to be too much for him.

Worse, he'd agreed to bring Jessie along tonight, and his daughter was currently chattering like a little magpie, telling Melanie all about her best friend at school and the accident she'd had with a pot of paste that had necessitated getting her hair cut very, very short.

"I'm glad that didn't happen to me," Jessie said. "I'm never getting my hair cut."

Melanie laughed. "You might reconsider that when it gets so long you're sitting on it and it takes hours and hours to dry."

Jessie fell silent, her expression thoughtful as she studied Melanie. "Your hair's long."

"Not that long," Melanie said. "Just long enough for me to braid it or pull it into a ponytail when I don't have time to do anything else with it."

"Daddy puts my hair into a ponytail sometimes, but it's usually crooked," Jessie said, sounding forlorn. "I never had a braid."

Melanie chuckled. "Well, fixing hair requires a talent some men don't have. That's why they wear theirs so short."

"Hey," Mike protested. "I can do anything you can do."

Melanie regarded him with amusement. "Is that one of those challenges you're so fond of?"

The memory of another challenge, one she'd issued very recently, slammed into him and made the temperature in the car climb by several degrees. And he'd foolishly trumped her just last night with that no-kissing, no-touching nonsense. It promised to be a very long evening and with Jessie along, there would be no relief at the end of it.

"I think maybe we ought to call it quits when it comes to making challenges," he said in a choked voice.

"What's a challenge?" Jessie asked.

"It's like a dare," Melanie told her.

Jessie's expression brightened. "Like when Kevin Reed dared me to climb to the top of the jungle gym?"

Mike felt his heart drop. "Please tell me you didn't do it?"

Jessie gave him an unconcerned look. "Kevin's dumb. I wouldn't do anything he said."

"Thank God," Mike murmured fervently. "Maybe we should change the subject."

Melanie regarded him knowingly. "Any particular topic you'd find a bit safer?"

"Yeah. Let's decide how we're going to get away from here tonight before dessert."

"Daddy!" Jessie protested. "We have to stay for dessert. It's the best part."

"It certainly is," Melanie agreed.

"But it's usually accompanied by lots of questions

everyone's been too polite to ask up until then,'' Mike reminded her.

Melanie frowned. ''You have a point. However, it would be rude to try to duck out. We'll just have to be evasive.''

''You did say you'd met Pam the steamroller, right?'' he inquired.

''I can handle Pam, now that I've seen her in action,'' Melanie foolishly insisted. ''I'm prepared.''

''Ha!''

She gave him one of those superior female looks designed to make men feel like idiots. ''Watch and learn.''

Mike barely contained a groan. This was one time he really didn't want to be right, but he knew Pam. If she was tricky on her own, she was the queen of sneakiness when she had Jeff around for backup. He and Melanie were doomed, no question about it.

The front yard of the Clayborne house was littered with toys. Melanie had to weave her way through bicycles, wagons and an obviously pricey miniature convertible—to say nothing of basketballs and beachballs—to get to the front door, which was already standing open. Pam was waiting on the front steps.

''Sorry about the chaos,'' she said, coming forward to give Melanie a hug as if they were old friends. To Mike, Pam offered a smug, told-you-so grin and a peck on the cheek. ''The kids aren't required to put everything away till they come in for the night and, believe me, they always wait till the very last minute.'' She leaned down to scoop up Jessie. ''How's my girl?''

''I'm fine,'' Jessie said, clinging to Pam's neck. ''Where's Lyssa?''

''She's in her room, expecting you. Wait till you see

her new dollhouse. Go on up,'' Pam said, setting her down at the foot of the stairs. "I'll call you when the pizza gets here.''

"The kids are having pizza?'' Melanie said wistfully.

"It'll keep 'em out of our hair,'' Pam said. "We can get to know each other.''

She grabbed Melanie's hand as if she feared Melanie might bolt. "You can come in the kitchen and talk to me while I finish the salad. And Mike, Jeff's out back waiting for those steaks.''

Mike nodded, then leaned down to whisper in Melanie's ear as he passed. "Divide and conquer. Told you she was sneaky.''

"I heard that,'' Pam said.

"I meant for you to,'' he responded happily. "I want you to know we're on to you.''

Melanie reluctantly followed Pam into a large, bright combination kitchen and family room with a huge island in the middle and windows all around. It was obvious that the family spent a lot of time here. There was a cozy built-in breakfast nook that was big enough for six, and at the opposite end a comfortable sofa sat in front of a fireplace. A giant-screen TV was angled toward the sofa, but could be seen from the kitchen as well. It was a great setup for having the guys over for football. In the kitchen itself, there were professional-grade stainless-steel appliances that Melanie's sister would envy.

"You must like to cook,'' she said to Pam.

"Actually I hate it,'' Pam responded. "But with five of us, I have to do it, so I figured I might as well create a space I'd enjoy.''

"You help Jeff with the nursery?''

Pam's expression immediately brightened. "That's how we met. I love plants. When I first came to town—

right after I got out of college with a degree in horticulture—his dad hired me.''

''And it was love at first sight?'' Melanie asked.

Pam laughed at her assessment. ''Hardly. With my fancy degree, Jeff thought I was a know-it-all. He used to tell me book learning wasn't nearly as important as practical experience. He'd grown up in the business and thought he'd seen just about everything. Then one very expensive garden died just days after he'd put it in, and he had no idea why.''

''Let me guess. You told him why.''

''Of course not,'' Pam said airily. ''I let him sweat. He worried and fretted and flatly refused to ask for my help, so I just kept on doing my job and keeping my mouth shut. After about a week the customer came in and started raising a ruckus about throwing all that money down the tubes. She threatened to go to another nursery if we didn't fix the problem pronto. Jeff was about to offer her a refund, when I took pity on him and stepped in.''

''What did you say?''

''That she'd be making a huge mistake going to anyone else, because she'd just have the same problem all over again. I'm not sure who was more surprised, the customer or Jeff, but he caught on right away.''

''Did he know what you'd figured out?''

''Of course not,'' Pam said with a grin. ''But he told her that I was their resident expert, and I knew how to solve the problem.''

''Which you did and saved the day,'' Melanie concluded.

''Pretty much. I'd seen some of the plants Jeff had dug out of the ground. Their root systems were being destroyed. We got rid of the little underground critters that were dining on them, and the next plants we put in thrived. That night Jeff asked to borrow a couple of my textbooks. We started having study dates and eventually concluded we made a pretty good team.''

She beamed at Melanie. ''And here we are ten years later, happy as can be.''

''Sounds like a match made in heaven,'' Melanie said, unable to keep the wistful note out of her voice.

''It is,'' Pam agreed, then seized on the opening Melanie had inadvertently given her. ''So what about you and Mike?''

''What about us?'' Melanie responded evasively.

''What kind of match are you?''

''The impossible kind,'' Melanie said at once.

''I know he has all sorts of baggage where his ex-wife is concerned,'' Pam said, ''but what about you?''

When Melanie said nothing, Pam added, ''Am I being too personal?''

''Pretty much,'' Melanie told her, hoping that would put an end to the subject.

''Sorry,'' Pam apologized, though she didn't sound particularly sincere. ''How serious is this baggage of yours? An ex-husband?''

Melanie chuckled despite herself. Pam obviously wasn't a quitter. ''No,'' she told her. ''No ex-husband.''

''Ex-boyfriend, then?''

''Something like that.''

Pam's eyes widened. ''Ex-*girlfriend?*''

''Heavens no!''

''Then what *did* you mean?''

Melanie thought about responding honestly but finally decided she didn't know Pam well enough for that sort of personal exchange of information. ''It's not worth talking about,'' she said eventually, and for the first time realized it really wasn't. Jeremy was the one with the problem. That didn't mean her issues would vanish overnight, but she was gaining some perspective, realizing the whole experience had taught her some home truths about her judgment skills.

Pam regarded her sympathetically. "I know I'm prying, but it's only because I care about Mike."

"So do I," Melanie admitted softly. It was the first time she'd allowed herself to say even that much about her feelings for Mike.

"Then I don't see the problem," Pam said. "There's obviously a powerful attraction at work here. Why not play it out?"

"Too much baggage on both sides," Melanie said succinctly. Mike's had made him reticent and gun-shy. Hers had made her aware of her own shortcomings. In such an environment it would be all but impossible for trust to flourish. It was not, she cautioned herself, a combination destined for happily-ever-after.

"But that's old news," Pam insisted. "You can both make a fresh start."

"Maybe neither of us wants to," Melanie responded.

"You'd rather wallow in your misery the way Mike has been doing ever since he and his wife split up?"

"I don't want to wallow in it," Melanie insisted. "But I do hope to learn something from it."

"How will you know if you've learned anything if you don't put yourself back into the game?" Pam demanded.

"I honestly don't know," Melanie admitted.

"I think what you both need is a little nudge from some good friends," Pam concluded just as the men came in with the steaks.

"Give it a rest, Pam," Mike said tersely, his worried gaze on Melanie.

Melanie forced a smile. "We're just indulging in a little girl talk."

"Ha!" Jeff muttered, giving his wife an affectionate peck on the cheek. "Pam's on a mission. Mike's been her personal project since the day he hit town. How many women have you tried to fix him up with, sweetheart?"

"*Tried* being the operative word," Mike said. "I've never said yes."

"Not even once," Pam confirmed, looking disgusted. "He's ruining my track record. I did very well with some of Jeff's other bachelor friends."

"What have I always told you?" Mike asked.

"That you'd find someone on your own when you were ready," she said. Her gaze narrowed as she looked speculatively from him to Melanie and back again. "Have you?"

Mike laughed, even as Melanie's heart did a little flip-flop.

"Nice try, darlin'," he said. "Now let's eat before the steaks get cold."

He snagged Melanie's hand and rubbed his thumb reassuringly across her knuckles as he led the way to the table. "Sit next to me," he requested, pulling out a chair. "That way I can protect you when Pam gets another bee in her bonnet about our relationship."

"I think Pam's done for the night," Jeff said, giving his wife a pointed look.

"Hardly," she retorted. "But I will give it a rest until dessert. I made a triple-threat chocolate cake. It's been known to make grown women weep and even a few men. It's also a great incentive for getting people to talk.''

"I hate chocolate," Mike declared.

"Liar," Pam accused with a grin. "Last time I made it, you told me all sorts of secrets just to get a second slice."

Melanie chuckled at Mike's stunned expression.

"You used that cake to wheedle information out of me?" he asked incredulously.

"Of course," Pam confessed.

Mike turned to Melanie. "Told you we needed to get out of here before dessert."

"For a triple-threat chocolate cake, I think I'll take my chances," Melanie said.

"Your funeral," he muttered darkly.

More than likely, Melanie thought. But she didn't have to reveal anything she didn't want these three people to know. She could have her cake and keep her secrets, too.

But gazing into Mike's eyes, feeling the faint beginnings of the same heat he'd stirred in her a few nights ago, she was beginning to wonder why she felt it necessary.

Chapter Eleven

Mike couldn't recall the last time he'd felt so relaxed or spent such an enjoyable evening with friends. Even Pam's persistent questions hadn't fazed him after a while, probably because Melanie had taken them in stride and fended them off with considerable aplomb. She'd gotten through a huge piece of Pam's triple-threat chocolate cake without revealing a single secret. Since he'd hoped for a few more insights into her relationship with the married man who'd betrayed her, he'd found that a little frustrating, but he had to admire her clever avoidance tactics.

Carrying a sleeping Jessie out to the car at midnight, he was struck by how right it all felt. He couldn't think of a single time during his tumultuous marriage that he'd experienced such a sense of contentment. After the first months of their marriage, Linda had flatly refused to socialize with their old friends, no doubt because she preferred doing drugs in private. It had isolated them, making it that much harder for him to adjust once the breakup happened.

Knowing—from bitter past experience and from Melanie's own commitment to leaving—that the contented feeling wouldn't last made him suddenly edgy and silent.

"What's wrong?" Melanie asked eventually as they neared her cottage.

"Nothing."

She regarded him with obvious impatience. "Come on, Mike. You had a smile on your face not fifteen minutes ago, when we left Jeff and Pam's. Now you look as if you've just received the worst possible news."

"In a way, that's exactly what happened," he admitted. "I realized that this entire evening was phony."

She stared at him incredulously. "What on earth is that supposed to mean?"

He struggled to put his emotions into words, something he usually avoided at all costs. "There we were," he began, "pretending not to be a couple."

Melanie nodded. "Which we aren't."

He regarded her bleakly. "Yet everything felt as if we were. Jeff and Pam could see it, too. They won't let me hear the end of it. Pam's going to want us to announce a wedding date soon. It's just the way she is. She's happy, and she wants everyone around her to be happy, too. She's convinced marriage is the key."

Melanie's expression faltered. "Oh, Mike, I'm sorry. I hadn't thought of it that way, but you're right. I should never have agreed to go to dinner. It just added fuel to her already overactive imagination, didn't it?"

"Yes, but that's not the worst of it," he admitted.

"Then what is?"

He wasn't sure he wanted to lay his own emotions so

bare, so he settled for asking her, "You enjoyed it, didn't you?"

"Except for dodging some of Pam's questions, yes," she admitted candidly.

"It felt right?" he prodded. "Comfortable?"

"Yes, it did."

He pulled into her driveway, cut the engine and turned to face her. "Does that make as little sense to you as it does to me?"

"Which part? That we enjoyed ourselves or that we're fighting it?"

"Either one."

Melanie stared straight ahead for so long, Mike was sure she didn't intend to answer, but she finally turned and met his gaze.

"It's where we are," she said quietly. "We can't change that. We're both trying to be as honest as we know how to be."

"Maybe we should try to change where we are," he persisted. It was something he'd never thought he would say. He'd never imagined that he would reach a point when he might be willing to risk his heart again, but to have the feelings he'd experienced tonight last forever, maybe it would be worth it. Melanie wasn't Linda. Far from it. She was strong. Maybe this time things wouldn't fall apart, if they recognized what they had and fought like hell to keep it.

"Can you do that?" she asked doubtfully. "Can you put aside the past and move forward?"

He wasn't sure. He wanted to, but he was as terrified as she obviously was. "Frankly, I've never tried before, but I'd like to," he admitted. "You?"

"I don't know if I can, Mike," she whispered. "I just don't know. It's not just you I'm not sure about. In fact, it really has nothing to do with you. It's my own judgment I don't trust.''

''Aren't you even willing to try?'' he asked. ''What we have is too precious, too rare, to turn our backs on it, just because we're scared. You were with that married man for how long?''

''Six months.''

''I was with Linda for a couple of years. I'd vowed to stick by her in sickness and in health, for better or for worse. For nearly a year of that the marriage was a disaster. It was the worst. If I can try to put that behind me, surely you can move beyond a few months with a guy you obviously never knew very well.''

''You make it sound so easy, as if we can just snap our fingers and all those pesky hurts and bad choices will disappear.''

''I know they won't disappear,'' he said impatiently. ''But maybe it's possible to put them in perspective, to leave them in the past.'' He gave her a penetrating look. ''Or are you still hung up on the guy? Is that what's really going on?''

''Absolutely not,'' she said so fiercely he had to believe her.

''Then why are you hesitating? I'm not suggesting we run off and get married tomorrow, just that we work on what we have, see where it could take us.''

''I still have to go back to Boston,'' she said with a trace of stubbornness, ignoring the rest. ''That hasn't changed.''

Mike wanted to pound his fist on the steering wheel in frustration, but he didn't. He merely asked, ''Why? What's holding you there?''

She hesitated, as if she weren't quite certain herself, then said, ''My family. My roots.''

"You have roots here, too," he reminded her.

"I have memories," she corrected. "It's not the same thing."

Mike stared at her silently, aware that he'd lost. Whatever she'd left behind in Boston—and he didn't believe for a minute it was as simple as family or roots—was more important than what she'd found here. And he couldn't continue pushing, couldn't continue fighting a losing battle, not with Jessie's heart to consider along with his own.

"I guess that says it all, then," he said finally. "Come on. I'll walk you to your door."

She looked almost as miserable as he felt. "You don't need to do that," she said stiffly.

"I'll walk you to the door," he repeated, climbing from the car and going around to yank open the passenger door with considerably more force than necessary.

Only when Melanie was standing next to him, with the moon casting light on her cheeks, did he notice the tears. He brushed them away with the pad of his thumb and felt his heart wrench.

"This is wrong," he murmured, right before bending down to kiss her. Even as he spoke, he wasn't entirely certain what he meant...the kiss, the unnecessary parting, any of it.

Because he wasn't sure, he didn't let himself sink into the kiss the way he wanted to, didn't taste her greedily or linger long enough to make her moan. It was enough just to feel her respond, to feel her sway instinctively toward him, to feel her heat. All of that felt every bit as right as the rest of the evening had. How could she turn her back on that? How could *he?*

He sighed at the mess they'd gotten themselves into.

It was wrong to want her so badly, knowing that it couldn't be.

But, damn, no matter what she said, no matter what his head told him, it felt right.

Melanie was still shaking long after Mike returned to his car and his daughter and drove away. She put her fingers to her lips, which continued to tingle from that last, lingering, unexpected kiss.

There had been so much sorrow in his voice, so much pain in his eyes, and she was responsible for that. She'd only been honest, only told him what they both already knew, that whatever this was they were feeling couldn't last. Even so, she felt as if she'd ripped out his heart.

And her own.

Why else would she feel so miserable if she hadn't fallen just a little bit in love with him?

"That can't be," she said fiercely, denying the feelings that bubbled up inside of her every time she thought of him.

There was no one around to challenge the claim, so she accepted it, just as she'd used it to keep a firm distance between them. Refusing to acknowledge her feelings was enough for now. If she pretended hard enough that Mike didn't matter, then she'd be able to leave when the time came.

And it had to be soon, she warned herself. She couldn't let this situation drag out forever, for his sake and her own. If she'd made up her mind to go, then she needed to do it.

She'd barely closed the front door behind her when the phone rang. Grateful for anything that might take her mind off Mike, she grabbed it.

But when she heard her big sister's voice, she burst into tears.

"Mel, what's going on? Melanie, talk to me right this second," Ashley ordered when Melanie's sobs went on and on. "Dammit, do I have to get in the car and drive down there?"

That prospect dried the tears as nothing else could have. "No," Melanie whispered hoarsely.

"That's better," Ashley soothed. "Now tell me what happened."

"I think I'm falling in love with Mike," she blurted, mostly to hear the words aloud, to see how true they rang. Unfortunately, they sounded dead-on accurate.

"Well, hallelujah!" her sister said.

"But I can't be in love with him," Melanie protested. "It's absurd. I hardly know him. Besides, I don't live here. I live in Boston."

"Not at the moment," Ashley reminded her, obviously trying to suppress a chuckle. "As for it being too soon, sometimes it doesn't take all that long. Not when it's right."

"The last time I fell in love, it was all wrong."

"I'll say," Ashley said lightly. "But you're a smart woman. You learned your lesson."

"Did I? How can you tell? I can't."

"Are there things Mike's keeping from you?"

"Yes," she said automatically, seizing on the excuse. "What?"

Pressed, Melanie wasn't entirely sure she knew why she was so uneasy about his lack of openness. "He won't talk about his marriage, not in any kind of detail. He's only told me it's over, that his ex-wife was into drugs, so he divorced her and got full custody of Jessie."

"That sounds like a lot of information to me," Ashley commented. "Did you believe him?"

"Yes."

"Well then, what's the problem?"

"What if I'm wrong? What if there's more to it? What if he'd take her back in a heartbeat if she got her life straightened out?"

"And what if you're right to trust what he's telling you?" Ashley demanded. "What if it's all over and it's you he wants?"

"I thought you guys didn't trust him," Melanie reminded her, irritated that her big sister was defending Mike now.

"No, we just told you to be sure you'd gotten all the facts about his past up-front. Look, sweetie, we can't make this decision for you. You're the only one who can decide if you love him and if he's worth the changes you'll need to make to keep him in your life."

"He might be." Melanie thought of the way she'd felt when they'd made love. It hadn't been just about sex. He'd made her feel…cherished.

And tonight? Tonight he'd opened a part of his life to her by sharing an evening with his friends. That was something Jeremy the jerk had never done, because he couldn't, because she was nothing but a dirty little secret in his life.

There was Jessie, too. Despite his concerns, Mike was permitting Melanie to get to know his daughter, the most precious person in his life. She knew him well enough by now to realize that he would never have allowed that to happen if he hadn't trusted Melanie not to break his little girl's heart.

He was letting her, slowly but surely, into his life, but she couldn't say the same. She'd kept her secrets, tried to keep Mike away from her sisters, pushed him away when he'd tried to ask for anything more than the most superficial relationship. She was doing a damn fine job of trying to protect herself, but what had it gotten her? She'd fallen for him anyway. She could walk away, but her heart would still be broken.

"I'm an idiot," she said eventually.

"Never," Ashley said loyally.

"Mike wouldn't agree with you."

"Then he's the idiot."

"No, he's not," she said adamantly.

Ashley laughed. "If you're that quick to jump to his defense, I think you have your answer, baby sister. Now what are you going to do about it?"

Melanie leaned against the wall and slid down until she was sitting on the floor. "I wish to hell I knew."

"You'll figure it out," Ashley said with confidence. "If you need any help, all you have to do is call. We'll come down there and cut through all the nonsense until the answer's plain as day."

Melanie smiled. "I think I'll try to get this one on my own."

"You know we love you."

"That goes both ways," she told her sister.

"And something tells me you'll find room in your heart for Mike and Jessie, too."

Melanie was beginning to believe that herself. She just had to pray that it wasn't too late.

"When can we see Melanie again?" Jessie asked for the thousandth time over breakfast. It had been a week since Mike had left her at her door, tears on her cheeks, his own heart heavy. "I thought she was our friend."

"She is," Mike replied grumpily. He'd been having

a lot of sleepless nights, thanks to Melanie and her stubborn refusal to give the two of them half a chance. He wasn't inclined to cut her much slack this morning. He'd honestly thought she might call him by now, that she'd reconsider.

"Then why can't we see her?" Jessie persisted.

"What's this sudden fascination with Melanie?" he asked, although he already knew the answer. Melanie had captivated both of them. As for him, he'd been in a lousy mood ever since he'd made love to her, ever since he'd discovered he was half in love with her and then realized she was going to walk out of his life all the same.

"She's nice," Jessie explained, as if that was more than enough to inspire her undying loyalty. "And she's a girl. She knows stuff you don't."

"Such as?"

"She can braid my hair."

Mike stared at his daughter, bemused. "I didn't know you wanted your hair braided."

"Well, I do."

"How do you know Melanie can do it?"

"She told me," Jessie explained patiently. "In the car. Weren't you listening?"

He'd heard something about his crooked ponytails and long hair, but he'd obviously missed the implications.

"And she said we could paint my fingernails," Jessie added excitedly.

"You most certainly cannot!" Mike said, appalled. He hated seeing kids running around trying to look like grown-ups. Adulthood and responsibilities came soon enough. He wanted his daughter to be a child as long as possible.

Jessie's eyes promptly filled with tears. "Why not?"

"You're six years old!"

"It's just for fun," she wailed.

Mike stared at her helplessly. Braids? Painted fingernails? If he was this far out of his element when Jessie
was only six, how the devil was he going to cope with
the teenage years?

He'd sworn that, for his own protection, he wasn't
going to go near Melanie again. But it was a measure
of his devotion to his daughter that he was actually considering breaking that vow just so Jessie could have her
hair fixed the way she wanted it and get her nails
painted.

Ha! he thought sarcastically. He'd been looking for
the perfect excuse for days now. Jessie had just handed
it to him, all wrapped up in little girlie bows.

"I'll talk to Melanie after I drop you off at school this
morning," he promised with a good show of reluctance.
"If Melanie says it's okay, we'll stop by later. You two
can play beauty shop to your heart's content."

Jessie beamed, her tears forgotten. "Thank you,
Daddy."

If only he could end all her tantrums so easily, Mike
thought wistfully. If only the path to his own happiness
were so obvious.

Instead lately he'd felt as if the ground were shifting
beneath him, turning all of his determined resolutions
about avoiding relationships into chaos. He'd actually
begun wondering if maybe he should consider trying just
a little harder to convince Melanie to stick around.
Maybe her first response had been a knee-jerk reaction.
Goodness knows, he'd had a few of those himself since
he'd met her.

That was why he'd made it a point to avoid her in
recent days. He'd been afraid he'd utter the words, beg

her to stay and then decide ten minutes later that he
wanted to take the plea back. Better to steer clear of her
until he knew his own mind. Better to avoid a rejection
that would remind him all too painfully of the way he'd
felt when Jessie's mother had turned to drugs, rather than
to him or their daughter.

In the meantime, though, dropping off Jessie shouldn't
be a problem. If Melanie agreed to the visit, he'd never
have to set foot inside the house. And with Jessie underfoot, he wouldn't act on any wild urges to drag Melanie into his arms and kiss her until she relented and
agreed to stay in Virginia with him.

He could do this, he concluded. It was just a matter
of concentration and keeping his hands to himself.

Mike's plan pretty much went up in flames the instant
he set eyes on Melanie right after he dropped Jessie at
school. There were dark circles under her eyes, as if
she'd gotten no more sleep lately than he had. Her lush
mouth curved into a cautious smile that all but begged
him to kiss her.

"I was thinking about calling you," she said.

The words sounded forced. She'd uttered them only
after they'd stood and stared at each other for so long,
Mike had begun to feel awkward.

"Oh?" he said, not sure what to do with that bit of
information.

"I'm sorry about the way things ended the other
night."

"Oh?" He felt he was beginning to sound like an
idiot, but she seemed to be on a roll. He might as well
let her take the lead here. Maybe it would save his pride.

"I shouldn't have pushed you away," she said, "not

when what I really wanted was for you to stay and talk things out.''

He shook his head in confusion. ''You didn't push me away.''

Melanie laughed. ''Not literally, no—but the outcome was the same as if I had. You haven't been near Rose Cottage since then.''

Pride be damned! ''To be honest, I was thinking of calling you, maybe suggesting you put some nasturtiums in the garden. Did you know you can eat them?''

She grinned. ''Actually I did. My sister Maggie is a magazine food editor. She passes along all sorts of little oddities like that. Maggie might like it if I planted nasturtiums.''

''I'll see about getting some, then,'' he said, the awkwardness suddenly back.

''Did you come by for some other reason, or was this just about the nasturtiums?''

He shook off the daze he'd been in since setting eyes on her. ''It's about Jessie, actually.''

''Is she okay?''

''I suppose that depends on how important hairstyles are to you girls.''

She regarded him blankly. ''What?''

''She wants braids. She says you can do them.''

''Sure.''

''And painted fingernails,'' he added.

''I can do those, too,'' she said.

''Would this afternoon work for you? You know how kids are when they get an idea. They'll nag you to death until you give 'em what they want. Jessie's worse than most.''

''This afternoon would be fine.'' She studied him curiously. "Do you intend to stick around for this make-over?"

"Lord, no," he said, appalled. "Unless you need me to. Normally I wouldn't leave Jessie, but she's eager to come, so I don't think it will upset her if I take off."

Melanie laughed. "I think we can manage without having you underfoot. I have to admit, though, that I'm a little surprised. I thought you didn't want me getting too involved in Jessie's life, especially after what I said the other night."

He studied her intently while debating how to reply. He opted for the truth. "It's too late for that. She likes you. This was her idea."

Surprisingly, delight lit her eyes. "I'm glad. I like her, too."

"Be careful, okay? Kids get attached real easily."

"Adults, too, sometimes," she said in a tone that caught him off guard.

He searched her face but couldn't read anything in her expression. "What are you saying?" he asked cautiously.

"I'm still working that out," she told him.

A tiny spark of hope flared to life inside Mike, but he knew better than to fan it into a full-fledged blaze. "Let me know when you figure it out, darlin'."

"Believe me, you'll be the first to know."

He met her gaze and saw the longing there. Eventually he nodded. "See you later, then."

She smiled slowly. "See you later."

"About three-thirty."

"That'll be good."

He couldn't seem to get his feet to move, couldn't seem to tear his gaze away.

"Is there something else?" Melanie asked, amusement lurking in her eyes.

"Nothing." He forced himself to turn away.

He was pitiful, he chided himself. Pathetic. He was acting like a lovesick kid who was scared to make a pass. Then again, so was she. The realization made him grin. By the time he reached his truck, Mike was laughing. Maybe coming here hadn't been such an idiotic move after all.

Chapter Twelve

After a trip to the drugstore for a selection of nail polish, Melanie sang along at top volume with an oldies
radio station as she gathered the rest of the essentials for
Jessie's makeover. It was the first time in practically
forever that she'd felt completely carefree. Maybe this
beauty day for Jessie was just what Melanie herself had
been needing, too—a chance to focus on someone else's
needs for a change. She remembered how much fun she
and her sisters had had when they were Jessie's age,
playing dress-up and using their mom's makeup. It had
been their favorite rainy-day activity.

Melanie was still singing, making up words when she
didn't know them, when the phone rang. She cut the
blasting sound on the radio as she picked up the receiver.

"Hello."

"Is this Melanie D'Angelo?" an unfamiliar voice
asked.

"Yes."

"This is Adele Sinclair, the principal at the elementary school. I'm really sorry to bother you, but this is a bit of an emergency. It involves Jessica Mikelewski."

Melanie's heart began to pound. An emergency? Involving Jessie? Why on earth would the school be calling her? "What's wrong? Is Jessie okay? Have you contacted her father?"

"She's had one of her incidents," the principal said, her tone dire. She seemed to expect Melanie to understand the implications.

"Incidents?" Melanie asked. "What does that mean?"

"In a nutshell, something upset her and she threw a tantrum. We can't get her to settle down."

Even as Ms. Sinclair spoke, Melanie could hear a child's pitiful wails in the background. Even though Mike had told her about Jessie's behavior problems, even though she'd witnessed a couple of the little girl's tantrums firsthand, it had been weeks since there had been any such incidents, at least none that Melanie was aware of. Maybe Mike hadn't mentioned them because he'd come to take them in stride.

"I've tried to reach her father," the principal continued, "but his cell phone is apparently out of range. Jessie's been crying for you. Normally we wouldn't contact someone we don't know, especially since you're not on the emergency list Mr. Mikelewski gave us, but Pam Clayborne, who is on the list, said she thought it would be okay for me to call you. I can't release Jessie to you, but could you please come over here and see her? It might help to calm her. Otherwise, Mrs. Clayborne said she'd come."

"I'll be there in five minutes," Melanie promised,

even though there were a million and one questions on the tip of her tongue. She could ask them once she'd seen for herself how distraught Jessie was, and after she'd done what she could to soothe her.

The weather had turned cloudy and chilly, so she grabbed her sweater, along with her purse and car keys, as she ran out the door.

The school was less than a mile away. She knew the location thankfully, because she and her sisters had loved going to the playground there as children. Her grandmother had taken them often. The big, old-fashioned three-story brick building was as solid today as it had been when it was built at least a half century earlier. There were new swings and other colorful equipment for the kids now, but at the moment no one was using any of it.

As soon as Melanie reached the main entrance, she could hear the same choking sobs that had echoed on the phone. She followed the sound to the principal's office.

The instant she opened the door, Jessie's small body hurtled into her. Melanie knelt down and held the little girl, murmuring soothing words even as she gazed up at a distraught woman who was undoubtedly Ms. Sinclair. She gave Melanie a sympathetic look.

"I'll give you some time alone with her," the principal murmured, obviously relieved. She retreated toward her office. "Meantime, I'll try again to reach Mr. Mikelewski."

Melanie nodded.

Jessie's arms clung to her neck, and her body quivered with sobs.

"Shh," Melanie soothed. "It's okay, sweetheart. I'm here now. Can you tell me what happened?"

Jessie shook her head.

"Why don't we sit on this bench over here?"

"No," Jessie wailed. "I want to go home."

"Baby, I can't take you home."

"Why not?" Jessie murmured into her neck.

"Because the school can't let you leave with me. They don't know me."

Jessie stared at her with tear-filled eyes and damp, blotchy cheeks. "But I do," she protested. "I told 'em you were my friend."

"I'm afraid that's not good enough. We need to wait for your dad. In the meantime, if you'll tell me what upset you, maybe I can help." Without asking again, Melanie scooped Jessie up and settled on the bench with the child in her lap. Slowly Jessie's tense little body began to relax against Melanie, but she still refused to say a word.

"Did something happen in class?" Melanie prodded, wanting to get to the bottom of whatever had set Jessie off.

"No," the child whispered.

"On the playground?"

Jessie's head bobbed, but she didn't look at Melanie.

"Did you have a fight with one of your classmates?"

Again, a faint nod.

Melanie took a wild stab in the dark. "Kevin Reed?"

Jessie pulled back, her eyes widened in shock. "How come you knew that?"

"It doesn't matter. Did he do something to you?"

Jessie sniffed. "He said I was a baby."

"Why on earth would he say something like that?"

"'Cause my daddy brings me to school and waits for me after. I *like* it that Daddy comes with me. It doesn't make me a baby, does it?"

"Oh, honey, there's nothing wrong with that at all. I'm sure lots of moms and dads bring their kids to school. Kevin's just being mean." Melanie couldn't help thinking that there was more to this than a bit of name-calling. "Did something else happen?"

"Uh-huh," Jessie admitted.

"What?"

"Kevin's dad doesn't bring him to school. That's why he was being mean to me," Jessie said knowingly. "He doesn't even have a dad. I said that, and then he hit me, and he said I didn't have a mom and that was worse."

Oh, boy, Melanie thought.

Jessie gave her a pleading look. "Can you be my mom? Please?"

"Sweetie, I wish I could be. You're a wonderful girl, and anyone would be lucky to be your mom...."

"Then how come my real mom left us?" Jessie asked plaintively.

"I don't think it was something she wanted to do," Melanie replied, feeling her way through the minefield. "I'm sure it made her very sad."

"Then why didn't she stay?"

"Because she couldn't," Melanie said, though she couldn't imagine such a thing herself. She tried to explain anyway, hoping she could find words that would reassure Jessie and wouldn't be too far from the truth or at least whatever version of the truth Mike had shared with Jessie. "Sometimes adults have to do things that are very painful, but they don't see any other choice. That doesn't mean your mom didn't love you. I'll bet your dad's told you that."

"I suppose," Jessie conceded grudgingly.

"If he said it, you can believe it."

''My real mom's never even come to see me. I'd rather have you as my mom,'' Jessie said fiercely.

The ache in Melanie's heart nearly overwhelmed her. She was completely out of her depth. It didn't help that she knew she, too, was going to abandon this precious little girl.

''It's just not that simple,'' she said eventually.

''How come?''

''Because it's up to the grown-ups to decide if they want to get married.''

''Don't you like my dad?''

''Your dad's terrific,'' Melanie said honestly.

''I know he likes you,'' Jessie said with confidence. ''I think you should decide to get married, so you can be my mom.''

Melanie was impressed with Jessie's persistence, even as she tried to think of some way to deflect it. ''I hear you want me to fix your hair and paint your fingernails.''

Jessie's expression immediately brightened. ''Did Daddy ask you if I could come over today?''

''He did.''

''Is it okay?''

Melanie nodded, though she wasn't sure how Mike was going to feel about it once he learned of Jessie's fight at school. There needed to be some consequence for her misbehavior, as understandable as it might be.

''Then let's *go*,'' Jessie said urgently. ''I want to go now!''

''I'm not allowed to take you,'' Melanie explained again, but her words fell on deaf ears. Jessie's face clouded over and the tears began to fall again.

She was working up to another full-fledged tantrum when Ms. Sinclair emerged from her office. ''I reached Mr. Mikelewski,'' she said. ''He's on his way.''

Thank God, Melanie thought. She was doing the best she could, but it was obvious that it wasn't enough. Jessie needed her father. The little girl was once again clinging to her and sobbing as if her heart would break. Melanie rubbed her back and murmured nonsense words until at last Jessie closed her eyes and fell asleep, obviously exhausted by her outburst.

Melanie continued to hold and rock her gently. Eventually she heard footsteps running through the school corridor and knew instinctively that it was Mike. He came charging through the door and skidded to a stop, his expression frantic. When he spotted them, a sigh seemed to shudder through him.

"Is she okay?" he asked, hunkering down to brush a curl from Jessie's tear-streaked face.

"She wore herself out crying," Melanie said just as they were joined by the principal.

Mike stood and glowered at Ms. Sinclair. "What the hell happened?"

"I'm not entirely sure," the principal admitted. "She and Kevin Reed got into some sort of argument that erupted into a shoving match. I don't know any more than that."

"Where was the teacher?"

"On the other side of the playground. She got to them in seconds. Neither of them was physically hurt, but Jessie was far too distraught to go back to class."

Mike turned to Melanie. "Did she say anything to you about what happened?"

Melanie nodded. "I think we should talk about it somewhere else, though."

Mike looked as if he wanted to argue or maybe punch his fist through a wall, but he fought for control. "Okay, then, let's get out of here."

"Wait just a minute," Ms. Sinclair commanded. "As you know, this isn't the first time Jessie has had one of these episodes, Mr. Mikelewski. It's possible that she needs more attention than we can give her here."

Mike looked shattered. "What are you saying?"

"That I can't have her disrupting class again. If it continues to happen, other arrangements will have to be made."

"You're kicking her out of school?" he demanded, his expression incredulous. "She's six. She's not some teenage delinquent."

"A disruptive child is a problem no matter what the age," Ms. Sinclair said. "I'm not asking you to remove Jessie just yet, but I am warning you that it's a possibility."

"But she's been so much better," he said. "I don't understand this."

"I think I do," Melanie said, giving his hand a squeeze. "Let's go."

He nodded slowly, then reached for Jessie, cradling her against his chest with heartbreaking tenderness. When his tortured gaze finally lifted to meet Melanie's, he said, "I'll meet you at my place."

Melanie nodded, her heart aching for him. "I'll be right behind you."

Mike kept glancing back at his sleeping child on the way home. Jessie looked so sweetly innocent now, but he knew all too well what she was like when she was out of control. He'd been deluding himself that the worst was behind them. How could he even consider a future with Melanie, when Jessie required every bit of love and attention he had to give? Even Melanie would have to see that after today. Hell, maybe that was even the real reason she'd been hesitating and she'd just been too kind to say so.

He carried Jessie inside, took her to her room and put her in bed. She barely whimpered as he removed her shoes and tucked a blanket around her. As worn-out as she was, she would sleep for at least another hour or two. That would give him and Melanie a chance to talk. There was a lot of ground to cover.

When he went back downstairs, he found Melanie in the kitchen brewing a pot of tea.

"I hope you don't mind," she said. "I thought we could both use it."

"It's fine," he said, raking his hand through his hair. "Now what the hell happened back there, and how did you get involved?"

As Melanie described the incident on the playground, Mike fought off the desire to go and pummel little Kevin Reed himself. Obviously, though, the kid had just been lashing back. He couldn't have known how devastating his words would be to Jessie. Nor, likely, had she grasped how hurtful she was being when she'd reminded Kevin he didn't have a dad.

"Kids that age have no idea how powerful words can be. They're unintentionally cruel to each other sometimes," Melanie said, echoing his thoughts.

"It's my fault," Mike said.

"How on earth can you believe that? You weren't even there!"

"Not today. I meant I should have done something to force Linda to face facts and get herself straightened out. Then Jessie would have her mom in her life. Dammit, I should have done something," he repeated.

"Such as?" Melanie asked, her skepticism plain.

"What could you possibly have done that you didn't do?"

He sank onto a chair and regarded her with bewilderment. "I have no idea."

"You couldn't make her better if she didn't want to get better," Melanie reminded him.

How many times had he heard the same words from the counselor he'd seen at the time, from his attorney, even from Linda's parents? He knew they were all right, but he couldn't help thinking that there must have been something he could have done or said to get through to her.

"Maybe if I went to her now," he said, beginning to formulate a plan even he could see was desperate and doomed to failure. "Maybe she'd be ready to listen."

Melanie looked stunned. "Is that what you want, to get your wife back?"

"No, of course not," he said without hesitation. "I swear to you, that's the last thing I want. But I want Jessie to have her mom back. I want her to be the happy-go-lucky, carefree kid she deserves to be."

"She will be," Melanie assured him. "It will just take time and patience."

"You heard Ms. Sinclair. We're running out of time."

"Talk to the teacher. Explain the situation. Talk to Kevin's mother. Since she's a single mom, surely she'll understand and help to stop Kevin from tormenting Jessie about not having a mom. And if you can explain to Jessie how badly Kevin must feel about not having a dad, maybe you can avert another incident like this one."

"But if it's not this, it will be something else. And if it's not Kevin, it will be some other kid," Mike said. "Jessie doesn't cope well with disappointment. Anything can set her off. Not getting the color crayon she wants, not getting the teacher's attention the instant she wants it, not getting to go to a party. Everyday life is filled with endless possibilities for disaster.'' He lifted his gaze to Melanie's and saw that her eyes were filled with sympathy.

"I'm sorry," she said. "It must be so difficult for both of you."

"I'm just sorry you got dragged into it. You never did say how that happened."

"Jessie asked for me," Melanie said.

"Really?" Mike wasn't sure how to interpret that. Jessie trusted very few people. Her attachment to Melanie was obviously stronger than he'd realized, maybe too strong.

"When Ms. Sinclair couldn't reach you, she called Pam, and Pam said she thought you wouldn't mind if I at least came to the school to try to calm Jessie down." Melanie studied him. "Was that okay? Did I overstep?"

"Of course not. Thank you for doing that. I try never to be out of cell phone range when Jessie's at school, but sometimes I can't help it. Things have been going so well lately that I didn't think it would be a problem if I rode out to a new job site for a couple of hours."

Melanie regarded him sympathetically. "Mike, there's not a parent on earth who could be more caring and attentive than you are. Don't beat yourself up over this. Sometimes things just happen. I'm glad I was around and could help."

"At least you see now why I've shied away from relationships. I can't drag someone else into this situation. It's too unpredictable. Jessie's too volatile for me to expect someone else to take her on. Forget all that stuff I said to you the other night. You were smart to turn me down flat.''

Melanie gave him an incredulous look. "You think you and Jessie are too much trouble? Is that what you're saying? Do you honestly think that had anything at all to do with why I said no?''

"Isn't it obvious?''

"Not to me. Jessie has some problems, sure, but she's a wonderful, smart, funny little girl. Any woman would be lucky to have the two of you.''

"How can you say that after what happened today?''

"Because it's true,'' she said fiercely. "Good grief, Mike, no one's perfect. No relationship is smooth every second. There are bound to be bumps and heartaches and problems of one sort or another. As for kids, sooner or later they're going to stir up trouble, whether it's the terrible twos or the traumatic teens or sometime in between, it's a guarantee they're going to make parents want to tear their hair out. Getting through all that just makes the relationship stronger.''

He knew she was trying to be kind and reassuring, but he didn't buy it. People bolted when the going got tough. That was what Linda had done. She'd chosen drugs, convinced that they would give her the pleasure that her marriage didn't. He'd taken off with Jessie rather than fighting to keep their marriage afloat.

Maybe Melanie was made of sterner stuff. Maybe she would stick it out the first few times Jessie caused problems, but over the long haul? He doubted it. He sure as hell couldn't risk it. Besides, if he cared about Melanie at all, why would he put her through that?

"Look, Jessie will be waking up soon. Maybe you should go,'' he said stiffly.

Melanie looked for a moment as if she might argue,

but then she stood up and started for the door, her expression sad.

Mike thought he was going to get her out of there before she saw that his heart was breaking, but she turned back, then crossed the room and leaned down to press her lips to his. She didn't linger, but his pulse raced just the same.

"I'll be expecting Jessie after school tomorrow," she said quietly but emphatically.

He stared at her. "What?"

"She and I have a date for a makeover. Obviously today's a bad day. Even if she were up to it, she shouldn't be rewarded for bad behavior, so I'm changing the date till tomorrow. Bottom line, I'm not breaking that promise." She gave him a warning look. "And neither are you."

"Come on, Melanie," he protested. "You can't want to do that after all this."

"Yes, I can," she said. "In fact, I want to do it more than ever. Three-thirty, Mike. Don't stand me up." She gave him another hard look and added, "Don't disappoint your daughter."

Now there was the clincher, he thought, staring at her. She knew he wouldn't be able to disappoint Jessie, not ever. When had Melanie learned to push his buttons so cleverly?

"We'll be there," he conceded reluctantly.

She beamed at him. "I knew you'd see it my way."

And then she was gone, leaving him filled with the oddest sense that maybe, just maybe, he'd gotten it all wrong. Maybe, rather than scaring her off, today's mess had almost convinced her to stay.

He smiled despite everything. Wouldn't that be just about the closest thing to a miracle he'd ever had any reason to hope for?

Chapter Thirteen

Melanie was mad as spit by the time she got home from Mike's. The idea that Mike and Jessie were too much trouble, too undeserving of love, was ludicrous. The man was an idiot! A loving, doting father, but an idiot nonetheless! How could he even think that was the reason she didn't want to be with him? How shallow did he think she was?

She was muttering under her breath about his stupidity when she got out of her car and realized that Pam was sitting on the porch steps watching her with undisguised amusement.

"Something—or someone—upset you?" Pam inquired.

Melanie considered being discreet but chucked the idea. Maybe Pam could help her make sense of what had just happened. After all, she and Jeff were Mike's best friends. They'd known him and Jessie for years.

"Mike," Melanie said succinctly. "Who else?"

"He is a stubborn one, all right. What did he do now?"

"Did you know that he's convinced himself that he and Jessie are too much for any woman to take on? That's why he doesn't get involved with anyone."

Pam nodded slowly. "I'd guessed as much, though he's never actually admitted it to me. I suppose it makes sense, given what he's been through, first with Linda and now with Jessie's behavior problems."

"Why the dickens haven't you told him he's crazy?" Melanie demanded. "Someone needs to get through that thick skull of his before he ruins his life."

Pam chuckled. "I don't think hearing it from me is going to convince him. He thinks I'll say anything to get him to date again. He's going to need proof from a woman who's brave enough to ignore all of his No Trespassing signs." She regarded Melanie speculatively. "Are you that woman? Or has he already scared you off?"

Melanie sank down on the step beside her. That was the issue, wasn't it? Was she playing a game here or, after everything she'd told Mike about going, was she really willing to put her heart on the line? Her ambivalence had nothing to do with Mike and Jessie being too much trouble. They were wonderful. It was her own self-doubt that was keeping her from getting in any deeper.

"I honestly don't know," she finally admitted.

"Then don't get his hopes up," Pam advised. "If you do and then change your mind, it will destroy any chance he ever has of believing in love."

Melanie scowled at Pam. "Gee, pile on the pressure, why don't you?"

Pam regarded her with absolutely no evidence of pity

or contrition. "There's something you need to understand, Melanie. I like you. I'd like to be your friend, but
right now Mike's my first priority. He and Jessie have
been through enough. Jessie's a thousand percent better
than she was when they first got here, but as you saw
today, she still has her moments. Another upheaval in
her life could destroy whatever fragile progress she's
made. The same goes for Mike. Can you imagine what
it must have been like for him to have this darling little
child depending on him and to have his wife say—
through her actions, anyway—that they weren't
enough?"

"No, I can't," Melanie said with a sigh. She knew
all too well how badly rejection and betrayal stung.

An uncomfortable silence fell between them. The sun
had finally broken through the clouds, providing a faint
warmth against the earlier chill, but even so, Melanie
shivered.

Pam turned to her. "So, what's holding you back?
Why won't you let yourself get serious about Mike?"

"Long story."

"I've got time."

Melanie shook her head. "I really don't want to talk
about it."

"Was it that awful? Are you still in love with someone else?"

"Hardly," she said with undisguised bitterness. "I
just don't want you to know what an idiot I was."

Pam regarded her intently, then chuckled. "A really,
really bad choice, huh?"

"You have no idea."

"Does Mike know?"

Melanie nodded.

"That's good. Can I say one more thing before I go?"

Melanie doubted if she could stop her. "Sure."

"Mike could never be a bad choice. He's one of the best guys around, along with Jeff, of course."

Melanie grinned. "Of course."

"You'd be a fool to let him get away," Pam persisted.

It wouldn't be the first time in her life Melanie had been a fool where love was concerned. But there was no comparing Mike with Jeremy. Even she could see that.

Still…stay here? Because that was what loving Mike would mean. Was she ready to make such a drastic change in her life? Was she ready to trust—especially after only a few brief weeks—that this time she'd finally gotten it right? Six long months hadn't been enough for her to figure out that Jeremy was lying to her and cheating on his wife. She'd had to be slapped in the face with that one.

"Think about it. That's all I'm asking," Pam said. "Now I'd better get out of here before Jeff comes looking for me. He wouldn't be happy if he knew I was over here meddling again."

Melanie grinned. "I'm glad you came, though. After this afternoon, it was good to come home to a friendly face."

"If you ever need someone to listen, give me a call. I'm known for my excellent, if slightly biased, advice."

"I may take you up on that," Melanie told her.

In fact, before all was said and done, she had a hunch she was going to need all the advice she could get. She might even be forced to call in her sisters, though only as a last resort. When it came to love, they rarely agreed on anything. In fact, the only time they were all in complete agreement was when one of their own needed moral support. Then they banded together like a bunch of protective mother hens. It was a reassuring unity, but Melanie knew that in the end this decision had to be completely and totally her own.

"Heard Jessie had a rough day yesterday," Jeff commented when he and Mike took a break from planting shrubs around a new home.

"Pam, I suppose," Mike said. There were times—like now—when he regretted making hers the first name after his own on his emergency contact list at Jessie's school. At the time he'd filled out that form, though, she'd seemed like a godsend.

"Of course," Jeff confirmed. "She told me the school had called her, and then she stopped by to see Melanie on her way home."

Mike frowned at that. "Oh?"

Jeff gave him an apologetic look. "I know. I told her she needed to stay out of it, but you know Pam. She cares about you guys. She thinks she's looking out for your interests."

"I'm sure she does," Mike said dryly. Pam had a reputation for good intentions. Unfortunately, they sometimes went awry, like the time she'd fixed up a friend with one of the nursery's customers, only to discover afterward that the man was already involved with the woman's best friend. Needless to say there had been three people very unhappy with her over that one.

"Is Jessie okay today?" Jeff asked, wisely changing the subject.

"She seemed fine when I dropped her off at school." He still wasn't sure how to take the fact that she'd insisted he drop her off a block away, rather than in front of the door. Had she taken his advice to heart about being more considerate of Kevin's feelings or was she merely trying to prove that she wasn't a baby? He suspected the latter.

Still it had given him an odd feeling to sit in the car down the street and watch her walk that final block all by herself. Only when she was safely inside had he finally driven off, aware that they'd reached a milestone. Jessie was growing up, whether he liked it or not.

It was going to be even stranger to take her over to Melanie's this afternoon and leave her there for whatever pint-size spa day Melanie had in mind. Her cries for Melanie during the incident at school yesterday had shaken him. She'd never called out for anyone other than him before. Was that yet another sign that her world was growing or was it a warning that her attachment to Melanie was becoming too deep? He had no idea how to interpret it.

"Hey," Jeff said. "Where'd you go? Is there something you're not telling me?"

"Jessie's spending the afternoon with Melanie," he said.

"Is that some sort of a problem?" Jeff asked.

"I wish to hell I knew."

"You want those two to get along, don't you?"

"Of course."

Understanding finally dawned on Jeff's face. "But you're terrified Melanie will leave and break Jessie's heart?"

"Something like that."

"And yours?" Jeff guessed.

"Jessie's my only concern," Mike insisted.

"Liar. Who're you trying to convince? Me or yourself?"

Mike gave him a rueful look. "That one's gotten a little muddy."

"For what it's worth, I think you could do a lot worse than inviting Melanie D'Angelo into your life."

"That's the problem," Mike said wearily. "I've already done worse. I'm not sure I could go through that kind of emotional chaos again. And Melanie's not exactly jumping for joy at the prospect, so maybe it would be smarter not to pursue it."

"What if you don't have to go through any sort of chaos?" Jeff asked philosophically. "What if Melanie's as perfect as you think she is, and the future's filled with unparalleled happiness? Are you willing to miss out on all that because you're scared of history repeating itself?"

Unfortunately, Mike had lived with the kind of fear Jeff was describing for a lot of years now. He'd been acting on it, keeping away from the dangers of another failed relationship. Old habits were tough to break... even when the potential rewards were extraordinary.

"I guess I'll figure that out when the time comes," he told Jeff.

"Don't look now, pal, but the time has come."

Mike sighed heavily. Yeah, he'd heard the clock ticking himself.

Mike dropped Jessie off at Melanie's at three-thirty with a promise to be back after all the girlie stuff was over. Jessie had already raced to the bathroom to see the selection of nail polish and hair ribbons Melanie had set out. Mike, however, hadn't budged from just inside the door. His troubled gaze kept drifting down the hall as if he wanted to follow his daughter and make sure she was okay.

"You can stay, if you'd like," Melanie offered, her

sympathy stirring for him. It was plain as day that he was having trouble letting go.

"No way," he said, then drew himself up. "I'm sure she'll be fine."

"She will be," Melanie assured him. "And I have your cell phone number. I'll call if anything comes up that I can't handle."

He nodded. "When I come back, I'll bring that pizza you were talking about the other day, one loaded with everything," he promised. "Thanks for doing this for her."

"No problem," Melanie insisted. "It will be fun."

He finally made a move toward the door, then hesitated, obviously reluctant to leave. "Sometimes she needs a lot of patience, especially when she gets tired."

Melanie saw the genuine anxiety in his eyes and fell just a little bit more in love with him at that moment. At this rate, there was going to be no turning back, probably way before she was ready for any commitment.

She put her hand on his arm, felt the muscle tense, then relax. "We'll be fine," she assured him, echoing his words. "I won't lose patience with her."

"I know that. It's just that I don't leave her with strangers much."

"I'm hardly a stranger."

"I know and she wanted to do this. She was really excited when I told her it was still on. She was afraid you wouldn't want her after what happened yesterday."

"Mike, stop fretting. It's only going to be a couple of hours," she said. "We're going to be so busy the time will fly by."

"Two hours," he said as if he were clinging to the thought. "Make sure she knows I'll be back in two hours. I told her, but she may need to hear it again."

"I'll tell her."

He still looked uneasy. "Maybe I should stay, after all," he said. "I could work in the yard. She wouldn't even have to know I'm here unless something happens."

Melanie realized then that his concern ran much deeper than some sort of father-daughter separation anxiety. He'd spent six years devoting himself to Jessie and her behavior problems. Letting go was going to be as difficult for him as it was for her.

"If you want to do that, it's okay with me," Melanie told him. "But something tells me you need this break as much as Jessie does."

He rocked back on his heels, considering her words. "Yeah, I guess I do," he admitted.

He gave her a plaintive look that made her heart twist.

"She's growing up, isn't she?" he asked, his tone oddly sad.

Melanie bit back a grin. "She is, but she has a long way to go. She'll still be your little girl for a while yet."

He gave her a resigned smile. "I guess I'd better get used to this, though."

"Today's a good time to start," she told him. "I'll take good care of her. I promise."

Only after she'd watched him walk to his car and take one last glance back at the house did she fully realize the magnitude of what had just transpired. Mike Mikelewski had entrusted her with the most precious thing in his life.

Whatever doubts she'd been harboring about him or about her own judgment vanished. Seeing his heart in his eyes like that was all she needed. The last bit of protective wall around Melanie's heart crumbled. She was in love with him, and she'd been right…there was no turning back.

* * *

Mike couldn't figure out what to do with himself. He had two hours to kill, time he normally would have spent with his daughter.

He was barely out of Melanie's driveway when he was tempted to pick up his cell phone and call to see how the two of them were doing. He resisted the temptation, because he didn't want to look like more of an overprotective idiot than he had earlier.

He jumped when the cell phone rang. Heart thudding, he grabbed it, sure that calamity had struck already. Jessie had probably painted the bathroom with nail polish while he and Melanie were talking. Or she'd gotten hold of the scissors and chopped off her own hair. His imagination ran wild, until he realized the voice on the other end of the line wasn't Melanie's.

"Meet me at the Graingers," Jeff said without preamble.

"Now?" Mike asked, his heartbeat slowing to normal. "I just left there an hour ago."

"What's wrong with now? Jessie's with Melanie, right?"

"Yes."

"Then get over here."

Jeff hung up before Mike could ask what was so important that it couldn't wait till morning.

He made the twenty-minute drive to the Graingers, muttering to himself about his friend's call. When he'd left earlier, everything had been fine. There'd been no potential landscaping disasters on the horizon. When he arrived to find Jeff sitting on a log, gazing at the river, his curses escalated.

"What the hell's the big emergency?" he demanded.

"No emergency," Jeff said, regarding him serenely.

Mike stared at him. "Then what am I doing here?"

"Having a beer," Jeff said, holding one out for him. Mike ignored it. "Explain," he said tightly.

"I figured you'd be a little antsy by now, so I'm providing a diversion. I would have met you at a bar, but I figured you'd never agree to it."

"Are you nuts?"

"I don't think so. I'm in a tranquil setting, taking a break, having a cold one. What's crazy about that?"

Mike could have listed half a dozen things, but instead he sank down beside Jeff and accepted the beer. He might as well. He did have two hours to kill and absolutely nothing better to do with them besides worry.

"How did you know I'd be going out of my mind about now?" he asked.

"Intuition. That and the fact that you were all but twitching with dread when you told me you were leaving Jessie at Melanie's this afternoon. Man, you have got to chill about stuff like this. Do you want Jessie underfoot for the rest of your life?"

"She still needs me," Mike insisted. "She's only six."

"She needs to figure out she can do okay with somebody other than her dad, too," Jeff said.

Mike frowned. "I know that. I leave her with you guys sometimes."

"Long enough to run to the store. That's about it," Jeff said. "Lyssa's been begging for Jessie to spend the night, but you've refused to let her."

"She's too young for a sleepover," Mike replied. "Besides, those two get along great for a couple of hours and then they're at war. I don't want you all to have to deal with that."

"They fight. They get over it. It's what kids do.

Haven't you been around when my three start picking on each other?''

"That's different.''

Jeff stared at him over his bottle of beer. "This I've got to hear. How is that any different?''

"They're siblings.''

"And that makes the fighting easier to take?''

"No, but they're your kids,'' he said, knowing he wasn't making a lot of sense. If Jeff and Pam could handle it when their three were on a tear, then adding Jessie to the mix wouldn't faze them. Rationally he knew that. In his gut, it was harder to accept. Jessie was his responsibility, not theirs.

"We consider Jessie one of the family,'' Jeff reminded him. "We're perfectly comfortable putting her in a time-out if she misbehaves.''

Mike held up his hands. "Okay. Okay. She can spend the night some weekend.''

"This Friday,'' Jeff said, seizing the opening. "You can take Melanie out and have the whole night to yourselves.'' He winked. "You can have your own sleepover.''

It was definitely an intriguing possibility, but Mike wasn't sure how he felt about all of these people ganging up on him to get some distance between him and Jessie. Or to close the distance between him and Melanie. It was all moving just a little too fast.

"Don't even try to tell me that you're not going to take advantage of this opportunity I'm giving you,'' Jeff said. "You, Melanie, alone all night long.'' He dangled the prospect like a very tempting carrot.

Visions of making love to Melanie slammed through Mike. Jeff was right again. Mike could hardly turn that down.

"I'll talk to her about it when I get back over there. She may be convinced by then that the Mikelewskis are a bad bet."

Jeff rolled his eyes. "You're not giving Jessie nearly enough credit. Most of the time these days, she's a good kid. You've done a great job of getting her to this point. And, frankly, to everyone else it's obvious that Melanie is charmed by her."

"If you say so," Mike responded, though he still harbored his own doubts.

He glanced at his watch and was surprised to see that with the drive back to town and the pizza to pick up, he was actually going to be a little later than he'd intended. He waited for the anxiety to rush over him, for the desire to grab his phone to call and alert Melanie that he was going to be maybe ten minutes behind schedule. Nothing happened. No gut churning. No desperation. Just the comforting realization that Jessie was in good hands.

He grinned at Jeff. "I owe you."

Jeff nodded. "You do, indeed."

"I'm not talking about this weekend. I'm talking about making me see that I don't have to hover over Jessie every single instant."

"Then my work here is done," Jeff said, standing up. "Pam will be proud."

Mike stared at him. "This was her idea?"

"Of course. You sure as hell don't think I'm this sensitive, do you?"

Mike laughed, feeling more relaxed than he had in a very long time. "Come to think of it, no."

Chapter Fourteen

"I can't choose," Jessie said, her brow puckered in a frown.

She studied the row of bottles of pink, mauve, beige and red nail polish Melanie had accumulated. In addition to those she'd purchased the day before, there was quite a collection left from when Melanie and her sisters had visited as teenagers. Some were all dried up by now, but there had been a half dozen that were still usable. Some shades were brilliant and clear, some frosted. Melanie could understand why Jessie was having such a tough time deciding. She had a hunch, though, that it wasn't just the variety that was holding things up. It was evident that Jessie didn't want the afternoon to end. She'd hugged Melanie a zillion times and said she was having the "bestest time ever."

"I like 'em all," Jessie added, her expression wistful as she studied the nail polish.

Melanie grinned. "Well, I can't very well paint every nail a different color. You have to choose, and soon, too, or your dad will be back."

"What color do you like?"

Melanie held out her hands. Her nails were cut short and buffed but unpainted. "I'm not the best person to ask," she told the little girl. "I never get around to painting mine."

Jessie's eyes lit up. "We can do yours, too. I'll help."

Now there was a frightening idea, Melanie thought. She'd already noted that Jessie had more enthusiasm than finesse with a hairbrush and the lipstick she'd convinced Melanie to let her try. Who knew what she'd do with a bottle of nail polish?

"This is your day," she told Jessie quickly. "Besides, I've been working in the garden. My nails would get all messed up."

"Not if you wore gloves," Jessie said reasonably. "Pam has really pretty ones at the nursery. They have little flowers on 'em. I like 'em a lot, but she doesn't have 'em in my size."

"I'll give that some thought," Melanie promised. "But we're running out of time now. Your dad will be back soon, so you'd better choose a color, so your nails will be beautiful when he gets here."

Jessie crawled into her lap and gave the bottles lined up on the edge of the sink a closer inspection. "This one," she said at last, choosing a hot pink. "Pink's my very favorite color in the whole world."

No one would have known that given the way she'd lingered over choosing. The chili-pepper red had been in the lead for a while, Melanie thought with amusement. Melanie was considering that one for her own toes one of these nights when she had time for a pedicure.

''Then pink it is,'' she said as she gave the bottle a few quick shakes. ''Now give me your hand.''

Only when Jessie's little hand was tucked in hers did Melanie realize that Jessie had bitten her nails to the quick. Trying not to wince at the sight, she said mildly, ''You know, your nails would be much prettier if you didn't bite them.''

Jessie frowned. ''I can't help it.''

She would have jerked them away in obvious embarrassment, but Melanie wouldn't allow her to. ''Sure you can,'' Melanie said easily. ''I used to bite mine. You know what got me to stop?''

''What?''

''I kept thinking how pretty they were going to be when they grew out. Every time I started to bite a nail, I thought about that, and soon they were growing. That's when my mom let me use nail polish for the first time.''

Jessie finally relaxed again and regarded her with curiosity. ''How old were you?''

''Way older than you. Twelve, I think.''

Jessie looked incredulous. ''And you still bit your nails?''

Melanie nodded. ''Whenever I got scared.''

Jessie watched her painting each tiny nail and seemed to be considering what Melanie had just told her. ''Didn't you ever get scared again?'' she asked at last.

''Sure,'' Melanie told her, starting on the other hand. ''Lots of times.''

''What did you do if you couldn't bite your nails anymore?''

''I drew in a great big breath, like this,'' she said, demonstrating until Jessie giggled. ''And then I told myself I could do anything. I could get up in front of the class if I had to or I could climb the rope in the gym or

I could ace my math test. Pretty soon I began to believe in myself, and I never even thought about biting my nails again.''

Jessie nodded, her expression solemn. "I can do that. I can even beat up Kevin Reed, if he picks on me again.''

Melanie smothered a laugh. "No, you cannot beat up Kevin Reed,'' she said emphatically. "It will only get you into trouble, just like yesterday.''

Jessie sighed heavily. "Sometimes Kevin needs to get beat up.''

"Was he mean to you today?''

Jessie shook her head. "He found somebody else to pick on.''

"I see.''

"Janice won't hit back.'' She gave Melanie a hopeful look. "Shouldn't I hit him for her?''

"Absolutely not. Let the teacher handle Kevin.''

Jessie looked disappointed. Then she held out her hands to admire her new pink nails. "They look beautiful,'' she said excitedly. "I can't wait for Daddy to get back. Let me see in the mirror again. Is my hair still okay?''

"Your hair is perfect,'' Melanie assured her, lifting her up so she could see for herself. The lipstick was another matter, but Jessie seemed happy enough with it. Mike was probably going to have a cow.

Obviously satisfied with her own reflection, Jessie threw her arms around Melanie's neck. "I love you.''

Tears immediately stung Melanie's eyes. "Oh, baby,'' she whispered, hugging Jessie tightly and breathing in the little-girl scent of strawberry soap and shampoo. "I love you, too.''

For the first time in her life, Melanie felt needed. How

was she going to give this feeling up when the time came? She'd had no idea that all these maternal instincts had been lurking deep inside her, just waiting for a chance to emerge.

Why did she have to give up anything? The thought came from out of nowhere to plant itself in her head. Once there, she couldn't seem to make it go away. Of course, loving Jessie was one thing. Committing herself to a relationship with Jessie's daddy was something else entirely. And for all the warm and fuzzy feelings she was having right this second, she still wasn't sure if she was ready to take that next step.

Even if she were, Mike might have other ideas about what the future held. There was no point in deluding herself that she was any match at all for the fears and doubts he had about his and Jessie's worth to another person. Those doubts had driven his life for years now.

She was still holding Jessie, lost in all these mixed emotions, when the doorbell rang.

"Daddy!" Jessie shouted, squirming to get down. "I'll get it. Where's my feathers and shoes?"

Melanie handed her the boa she'd found in her grandmother's closet. It was shocking pink and Jessie had fallen in love with it on sight. She'd also claimed an old pair of red high heels from the closet.

"Remember, you have to walk slow in those shoes," Melanie reminded her.

"I will," Jessie promised.

Jessie tottered from the bathroom and left Melanie to wipe away any trace of tears from her cheeks before she went out to face the two people who could change her life forever.

Mike knew he was a goner when he came back to Melanie's at five-twenty with a large, deep-dish, everything-on-it pizza and found his giggling, bright-eyed daughter with her hair in an elaborate braid of some kind and bright-pink polish on her tiny nails. He could have lived without the lipstick, but gathered that was a necessary part of playing grown-up. She had some sort of feather thing wound around her neck and dragging on the floor behind her. She was wobbling in a pair of high-heeled shoes that were much too large for her. It was the most normal moment he could ever recall, and it made his heart ache that Melanie had been the one to share it with her and not him. But how could he regret anything that had made his baby girl so happy?

He looked at Melanie and mouthed a silent thank-you before scooping Jessie up in his arms and tickling her.

"You've gone and turned into a gorgeous grown-up lady on me," he said. "Where's my little girl?" He glanced at Melanie and asked with feigned ferocity. "What have you done with her?"

"No little girls here," Melanie teased. "Right, Jessie?"

"Just me, Daddy. But this is for when I'm at Melanie's," she recited dutifully, then gazed at him hopefully. "Can we come here all the time?"

Mike looked at Melanie and came to the conclusion he should have reached way before this. "That's something Melanie and I will have to discuss one of these days."

"Ask her now," Jessie prodded.

"No," he said firmly. "Now we have to eat pizza before it gets cold."

"But—"

"No arguments," he said firmly. "Or I'll have to call

Lyssa and tell her you won't be able to have a sleepover at her house tomorrow night, after all.''

Jessie looked awestruck. "I can spend the whole night at Lyssa's?''

"You can," he said, glad that Jeff had backed him into that particular corner. It was obviously something Jessie had wanted and had never dreamed he would allow.

"How come?'' she asked.

"I think you're old enough now, don't you?''

She bobbed her head enthusiastically, but then worry creased her brow. "Won't you be lonely, Daddy?''

Mike met Melanie's gaze and held it until her cheeks turned pink. "I don't think so,'' he said quietly.

"I got an idea,'' Jessie said excitedly. "Why don't you have a sleepover with Melanie?''

Mike bit back a groan. Out of the mouths of babes. "Don't worry about me,'' he told Jessie. "I can make my own plans for the evening.''

"But—''

He gave her a warning look. "Jessie!''

She sighed. "I just want Melanie to be my mommy,'' she said wearily. "I wish you'd hurry up and ask her.''

Mike glanced at Melanie and saw the bright-red patches on her cheeks and something that looked like panic in her eyes. She definitely wasn't ready to hear that he was beginning to think a lot like his daughter. He was ready to give Jessie the new mommy she'd been dreaming of.

She should never have agreed to go out with Mike tonight, Melanie thought, her pulse scrambling frantically and her stomach knotting. She was not ready to have the kind of discussion he clearly had in mind, especially when she was almost a hundred percent certain that his motives had nothing to do with love and everything to do with Jessie. He was going to dangle everything she'd ever wanted in front of her—a home, a family—and she was going to say no because he wasn't offering the most important thing of all, his love.

But maybe she was getting ahead of herself. Besides, it would be cowardly to back out. Maybe she'd gotten the signals all wrong anyway. Maybe he was really interested in nothing more than an entire evening for just the two of them. Maybe that glint in his eye had been about sex, not marriage.

She had almost convinced herself that it was as simple as that when he announced they were going to spend the evening at his place.

"I've got chicken slow-roasting in the oven," he told her, his gaze locked with hers. "I hope that's okay."

"It sounds perfect," she answered honestly. "I hope it's roasting *very* slowly."

He grinned. "I can always turn the heat down when we get there."

"And I can turn it up," she countered, enjoying the flare of desire in his eyes and relieved that there'd been no hints about serious talk for the evening's agenda.

They made the drive to his house in silence, but rather than feeling uncomfortable, Melanie was filled with anticipation that seemed to grow with each mile that passed. She'd missed being close to Mike, feeling his touch.

"Is Jessie settled for the night at Lyssa's?" she asked eventually.

"I hope so," he said, suddenly looking worried. "This is a big step for her."

"And for you," Melanie guessed.

He shook his head. "I know it's ridiculous, but she's been my responsibility for so long, it's hard to stop worrying about her."

"From what I hear about parents and kids, you'll never stop worrying about her," Melanie told him. "But you will learn to cope with it and keep it in perspective." She grinned. "I'll do my best to provide a distraction tonight."

"I don't think there's any question that you'll do an excellent job," he said, putting his hands on her waist and lifting her from the truck.

He looked into her eyes, then slowly lowered his mouth to take hers in a long, greedy kiss.

Melanie felt as if she were floating, which she was, she realized eventually when she could think straight again. Mike was still holding her off the ground, her body molded to his.

"Maybe you ought to put me down," she suggested lightly.

"I don't want to."

"We'll get inside faster if you do."

He laughed. "You do know how to create a powerful incentive, don't you? But I don't have to put you down to get inside."

Before she realized his intention, he'd put an arm under her knees and rearranged her against his chest. He set off toward the house in long, determined strides.

"Are you suddenly in a hurry?"

"Darlin', I've been in a hurry for this since the last time we made love."

She studied him curiously. "Why haven't you done anything about it?"

"Too many complications."

"And now?"

"I think we're getting them untangled."

Melanie wished she were half as sure of that as he seemed to be. But before she could express her concerns, they were inside, in his room and Mike was lowering her to his bed. The heat in his eyes was enough to melt away whatever crazy ideas she'd had about talking.

"Do you know how incredible it is that we have the whole night ahead of us?" he murmured. "I want to take this slow. I want to get to know every inch of your body. I want to watch you come apart in my arms time and again."

Melanie trembled at his words, at the gentle touch of his hands as he worked the buttons on her blouse until they were free and he could shove the material away. Then he skimmed his fingers over her lace-covered breasts until the peaks were tight, aching buds.

"You are so amazing," he whispered, his voice husky. "Amazing."

Melanie tried to find the words to respond, but her breath caught in her throat when he covered her breast with his mouth and sucked. Her hips rose off the bed in response to that incredible sensation.

"Forget slow," she said in a choked voice, writhing beneath him. "Slow's for next time or the time after that. I want you now, Mike. Please."

A smile spread across his face. "Well, when you ask so sweetly, how can I possibly say no?"

He stripped away her panties, pushed down his own pants and entered her in one hard thrust that filled her and took the last of her breath away.

Then he began to move, teasing her, tormenting her until the sensations were too much, too raw and needy. Her body felt as if it were on fire, as if it were one exquisite nerve that was wound so tightly it was destined to snap with one more stroke, one more caress, one more flick of his tongue across her feverish skin.

In the end that was exactly what sent her flying over the edge, his tongue on her nipple sending a shock wave through her that reached her toes. She screamed, but he caught the sound by covering her mouth with his own.

And as their breath mingled and their bodies came apart in perfect harmony, Melanie was filled with a joy so pure it uncomplicated everything. There was only this man, this moment and the waves of love washing through her.

It seemed like an eternity before Mike could move again. Melanie had worn him out in the most pleasurable way possible. He didn't care if he never budged from his bed again.

He felt an elbow prod his ribs and moaned. "Again?"

She laughed. "No, you idiot. Even I know my limits. What I'm after is food. That chicken ought to be way past done by now."

"It's probably so dried out, it's chicken jerky," he said.

"I'm not sure I care at this point."

He grinned at her. "You really are hungry, aren't you?"

"Starving. Mind-boggling sex will do that."

"Ah, flattery. You definitely know how to motivate a man," he said, reaching for her.

"I'm not trying to motivate you to make love again," she said impatiently, giving him a gentle shove. "I'm trying to get you out of this bed and into the kitchen."

"Then you used the wrong tactic."

She eyed him curiously. "What will work?"

"Mention the triple-threat chocolate cake that Pam sent over for us."

"Oh, my God!" Melanie said, scrambling past him to grab his shirt from the floor.

Mike watched her unabashed eagerness and laughed. "Since you're up, you can bring a tray in here."

"Dream on. That cake is mine," she said as she bolted from the room.

Laughing, Mike dragged on his pants and followed. By the time he reached the kitchen, she had her first forkful of cake.

"For me?" he inquired.

"I don't think so," she said, biting into it, then groaning with obvious ecstasy.

"Careful, or I'm going to think you like that better than sex," he scolded.

"It's a toss-up," she retorted.

"You're going to spoil dinner."

"I don't think so. I took a look at that chicken. It's a goner."

"Then I'll nuke a frozen homemade lasagna. How does that sound?"

"Great, but I'm not waiting for it," she said, pulling a chair out from the table and sitting down. His shirt rode so far up her thighs, Mike could hardly think straight. He simply stood and stared. She chuckled. "The lasagna?"

"What?"

"In the freezer," she prodded.

He sighed and turned to the refrigerator. A few minutes later, the meal—one of many prepared and provided by Pam—was heating. He put the salad he'd tossed earlier on the table, then took the fork and cake away from Melanie. She didn't protest. She just closed her eyes and sighed with pure bliss.

"I really need that recipe. I have to pass it along to Maggie, so she can use it in the magazine. She'll be worshiped by women everywhere as a chocolate goddess."

Mike chuckled. "Is that a goal of your sister's?"

"Not really, but a little adoration is always good for the soul."

"Do you want to be adored?"

"Not by hordes and hordes of people," she said thoughtfully. "Maybe by one person."

Mike wondered if now was the time to ask the question that had been spinning around in his head ever since he'd seen her with Jessie yesterday afternoon. It was as good a time as any, he finally concluded, searching for the right words.

"Jessie obviously adores you," he began.

Her head shot up and her gaze met his. "She's a great kid," she said, an unmistakable note of caution in her voice.

Mike plunged ahead. "I'm glad you can see past the problems and recognize that. Does that mean you'd consider something a little more permanent?"

Alarm flared in her eyes. "Such as?" she asked, her tone wary.

"Don't look so terrified. I'm not going to ask if you'd like to be her nanny," he said. "I was thinking more along the lines of her mom. Would you consider marrying us?"

She studied him for what seemed like an eternity. "Because it's what Jessie wants?" she asked eventually.

"No, because it's what I want, because I think you'd be happy here. I think I could make you happy here."

"You haven't said anything about love."

Mike hesitated. He knew women wanted the pretty words, but he didn't believe in love, even now. It hadn't done anything but cause misery in his life. His continued silence apparently spoke volumes, because Melanie shook her head and stood up.

"I need to go," she said, looking unbearably sad.

"Now?" he asked incredulously. "You want to leave now? Why?"

"Because this is never going to work. I see that now."

"What's not going to work? We've been making love for hours. I just asked you to marry me," he all but shouted.

"For Jessie," she reminded him. "Not for you or even for me. That's not good enough. I want more, Mike. I want it all. I didn't think I did. When I came here, I was just like you. I was sure love didn't exist, not the way it's portrayed in novels. Now I have this tiny glimmer of what it can be like, and I'm starting to believe."

He wished he shared her conviction. "I can't give you what you want," he said, his heart heavy.

But even as he said the words, even as he saw her slipping away, he saw what she'd seen…a future that was bright because they were together. He wanted to grab it. He wanted desperately to believe that everything was possible.

But Melanie was already running from the room, leaving him behind. It wasn't the first time a woman had left him, but this time it hurt even more.

For the first time ever, he knew the real meaning of despair and loneliness.

Chapter Fifteen

Mike knew he had to go over to Pam's to pick up Jessie, but he was dreading it. He knew there would be a thousand questions on the tip of her tongue, questions he flatly refused to answer. He wasn't sure he could bear to see the sympathy that was bound to fill her eyes when she figured out that Melanie had turned his proposal down flat.

Or maybe what really worried him was the possibility that she would laugh herself silly and call him an idiot when she realized he'd done it all for Jessie and offered nothing of himself to Melanie. He still wasn't sure what had kept him from laying his heart on the line. Fear, more than likely. It was the ever-present fear that had kept him from reaching out to anyone for a long time now.

Oddly, keeping the proposal all about Jessie didn't seem to be making the sting of Melanie's rejection one bit easier to take. That rejection was all about him and his inadequacies, just as Linda's abandonment had been. He wasn't enough for either one of them.

Even as he thought that, though, he knew how ridiculous it was. Linda hadn't left because he was inadequate. She'd left because the drugs were powerful and addictive. Period. As for Melanie, hadn't she really said that he *was* enough for her? He was the one who'd been unwilling to offer his heart.

Walking up to the Claybornes' front door, he drew in a deep breath and braced himself. Thankfully, it was Jeff who answered the door.

"You look exhausted. I'll take that as a good sign," Jeff said, putting a typical male spin on things.

"You shouldn't," Mike growled. "Where's Jessie?"

Jeff's gaze narrowed speculatively. "She's out back with Lyssa. They're swimming. It's a gorgeous day, in case you haven't noticed. I can loan you a bathing suit if you'd like to join us. Pam and I are about to have breakfast out there. There's more than enough for you, too."

"No, thanks," he said curtly. "I'll just find Jessie and get out of your hair. I'm sure you've had enough of her by now."

"Actually she's been a little angel," Jeff said, continuing to study him with a frown. "You're the one I'm worried about. What's up with the attitude? Didn't things go well with Melanie?"

Mike scowled right back at him. "Look, you did the sensitive thing once. That's enough. You're not that great at it."

They'd known each other long enough that Jeff didn't take offense. He merely shook his head. "Now I really am worried. Should I get Pam?"

"God, no!" Mike said. "Please be a pal—get Jessie and don't let on that anything's wrong."

"One look at your face will be all it takes for Pam to see that something's very wrong," Jeff warned. "Maybe you should go away and work things out with Melanie, then come back later."

"Not going to happen," Mike said. "Will you get Jessie or do I have to do it?"

Jeff looked as if he might poke and prod some more, but he finally shook his head. "Whatever you want, man."

Mike heard Jessie's screams of protest a minute later and sighed. He should have known it would be impossible to do this the easy way.

Before he could take a step in the direction of the backyard, Pam came through the house like a whirlwind.

"Why are you insisting on dragging Jessie off when she's having such a good time?" she demanded. "And what's with standing out here on the front stoop instead of coming around back and getting her yourself?"

Mike ignored the second question, because he figured Pam wouldn't like hearing that he'd been avoiding her. "I came to get my daughter because it's time for her to go home," he said tightly.

Pam studied him as intently as Jeff had. "Not when you're in such an obviously lousy mood," she said emphatically. "I'll go tell Jessie she can stay, then you and I are talking."

"No, we're not," Mike said just as emphatically. He relented on one point but not the other. "Jessie can stay, but you and I are definitely not talking."

Pam scowled at him. "Stay here," she ordered, then went to give Jessie the good news.

Mike stared after her, muttered a curse and turned on

his heel. Jessie was in good hands, and Pam was right about one thing. He was in a lousy mood. He needed to do something physical outdoors and work off some of his frustration.

Instinctively he headed for Melanie's, just as he had on so many other Saturday mornings lately. He didn't have to see her. Hell, he didn't *want* to see her. He could rip out a few more weeds, check on the progress of the plants he'd put in last week, spread around a little fertilizer, then hightail it out of there. With any luck Melanie wouldn't even be home.

But, of course, she was. He could feel her gaze on him, but she didn't come out of the house. When he couldn't stand the tension a moment longer, he sighed heavily, put his gear back into his truck and left.

Instead of soothing him, for the first time in his life the work had left him edgy and more miserable than ever. But he knew from bitter experience that when his heart was aching, the only answer was work.

Just because Melanie was abandoning him didn't mean he had to abandon their project. He would be back next week and the week after that, no matter how painful it was, because he'd made a promise to her and to her grandmother's memory. He didn't make a lot of promises these days, but the ones he made, he kept.

Melanie swiped angrily at the tears running down her cheeks. Why had Mike shown up here today? Was he deliberately trying to make her even more miserable than he had the night before? And where was Jessie? Melanie had grown used to having the two of them out there together, kneeling on the ground, heads bent close as Mike taught Jessie how to settle a young plant in the rich, dark earth. Jessie's bright-as-sunshine laughter had always had a knack for making Melanie's heart lighter. She could have used a little of that today.

But, of course, he wouldn't bring Jessie with him. His daughter would have too many questions about why her father and Melanie weren't even looking at each other, much less talking. That would have made an already tense situation unbearable.

So today he'd been all alone, working at a feverish clip as if he were trying to forget something. She sure as heck knew what he was trying to forget, the same thing that was tormenting her. Damn the man and his stubborn refusal to see what was right under his nose. She loved him. She'd done everything but spell it out to him, and he'd sat there insisting that his proposal was only about providing a mother for Jessie. Well, he could just take that notion and shove it.

When the phone rang, she snatched it up. "What?"

"You sound cheery," Maggie murmured. "Maybe I'd better call back when you're in a better mood."

"That could take weeks," Melanie told her sister.

"Uh-oh. What happened?"

"Nothing I want to talk about."

"Does that mean things aren't going so well with the sexy gardener?"

"He's not a gardener. He's a landscape designer."

"Whatever."

"Why are you calling? Is it just to annoy me?"

"Actually I was calling to let you know that there's a job opening here at the magazine. It's in marketing."

Melanie sank onto a kitchen chair. "You're kidding!" She wasn't sure which stunned her more, that Maggie had found the ideal job for her on a well-respected regional magazine or the fact that it would mean they'd be working together. Maggie liked having her own niche in the world. Of all of them, she'd always been the least likely to share. But she loved her sisters, and they'd always known that in a crunch she would do what she could for any one of them. This offer was proof of that.

"Not something I'd kid about," Maggie assured her briskly.

"Are you sure you'd be comfortable having me around?" Melanie asked.

"As long as you don't try to tell me how to run the food pages, we'll get along just fine," Maggie said in a dry tone that wasn't entirely meant in jest. "Come on, sis. This is perfect for you. It's one step above entry level, the number two spot in the department. Of course, there are only three people in the department, but that's even better. You'll get experience in every aspect of the marketing process. If you're interested, I can set up an appointment first thing Monday morning. If you drove back tomorrow, you'd have plenty of time for me to brief you about the magazine. I've already told the marketing director all about you. She can't wait to meet you."

"Does this mean I'd finally get a glimpse of that sexy photographer you've been going on and on about?" Melanie teased.

"Let's leave Rick out of this," Maggie said tartly.

Melanie tried to read her tone and couldn't. She'd thought Maggie was merely in lust with the photographer, but maybe there was more to the story than she knew. Whatever it was, she wasn't going to get it out of her tight-lipped sister.

But thinking of the reportedly hunky photographer made Melanie glance outside. Mike was gone. She barely contained a sigh. It was over between them, so why was she even hesitating? This was just the shove she needed to head back to Boston.

Still, she couldn't seem to make herself say yes to Maggie's offer. "I really appreciate this, but can I think about it, at least overnight? I'll call you first thing tomorrow morning. You can't do anything before Monday anyway, right?"

"Why aren't you jumping at this?" Maggie asked, obviously irritated that Melanie wasn't reacting with more enthusiasm. "Is it Mike?"

"Mike and I are over," Melanie insisted.

"Then I really don't see the problem," her sister said. "Are you worried about working with me? I'm telling you, it will be okay."

"I'll call you in the morning," Melanie said without offering the explanation Maggie so obviously wanted. Maybe she kept silent because she didn't have one, at least none that made a lick of sense.

She was still pondering the reason for her lack of enthusiasm at daybreak on Sunday. She was no closer to making a decision than she had been the day before, and maybe that was answer enough.

Fortunately, when she called home, Maggie was out. Melanie left her sister a message saying thanks but no thanks, then hung up before she could change her mind.

After that she sat staring at the phone for an eternity, wondering what on earth she'd just done. She'd turned down the chance to interview for her dream job. For what? A man who couldn't see what was right in front of his face? Staying on in a little town where job opportunities like this one might never come along?

Apparently so. She sighed. All she knew for certain was that she needed time—time to know her own mind, time for Mike to figure out his.

Then, if there was obviously no hope at all, she'd go back to Boston. This job might be gone, but there would be others. Much as she hated admitting it, given how furious she was with him, Melanie knew in her heart that finding another man like Mike wouldn't be nearly as easy.

Mike was beginning to question his own sanity. He couldn't seem to stay away from Melanie's. He was back in the garden every Saturday waiting for who knew what to happen. Maybe he was hoping that eventually she would get his unspoken message that he wasn't going anywhere.

He was actually surprised that she hadn't left by now, fled to Boston just to avoid the pain of seeing him, just as she'd fled here in the first place. There was obviously nothing holding her here.

Or was there? Had she started to see through his muddled proposal to what was in his heart? Had she figured out yet that he was too terrified, too vulnerable, to put himself on the line the way she expected, the way she deserved? He was obviously waiting for a miracle that might never come.

Jeff and Pam had been badgering him for weeks now to talk to Melanie and straighten things out. They still didn't know the whole story, only that whatever had happened had been his fault. He'd admitted that much.

Jessie was retreating into sullen silences more and more each time he refused to arrange a visit to see Melanie. Things had never been more tense between him and his daughter.

Why not just talk to Melanie and lay everything on the line? Mike asked himself. Surely he couldn't be any more miserable than he was now.

He woke on Saturday morning to brilliant-blue skies with not a cloud in them. The temperature was already in the mid-seventies by the time he dropped Jessie off at Lyssa's and got to Melanie's. His mind was made up. He was going to settle things once and for all today. It helped that all the plants were in the ground and flourishing. After today he'd have no more excuses for hanging around if she turned him down a second time. He'd even driven to Richmond the day before and picked out a ring. Surely that would show Melanie how serious he was.

Of course, planning the whole thing out and actually working up the courage to knock on the door were two entirely different things. The backyard might as well have been a million miles wide. Add in a moat and that was the width of the divide between them.

He remembered something his mother had once told him years ago when he'd been scared to try out for his high school baseball team. "Nothing beats a try but a failure." It had been her favorite saying, a message that sometimes people defeat themselves and that he should never allow himself to fall into that trap.

He knelt down to loosen the soil around the rosebushes, put a few stakes in the hollyhock garden, then tended to the foxglove and snapdragons. None of it was necessary, but it gave him time to gather his courage, all the while aware that Melanie was standing at the kitchen window, watching him.

"It's now or never," he told himself, but before he could move, he looked up and, like the miracle he'd been waiting for, she was there.

Melanie hadn't been able to bear it another moment. Every Saturday for weeks now, Mike had worked in the garden. He'd never brought Jessie again and he never announced his arrival. She would just look outside suddenly and see him there, the sun glinting off the threads of gold in his hair, his muscles straining as he worked.

If he chanced to look up and spot her, he waved, but that was all. He never smiled or beckoned.

Nor did Melanie seek him out. It hurt too much simply to see him, his big hands so gentle with the fragile plants he was tending. It hurt to know that those hands would never touch her with such tenderness again.

Today she had watched from the cottage's kitchen window and imagined his work-roughened hands on her skin, remembered the tenderness with which he'd coaxed responses from her body.

Maybe it was need or yearning, but suddenly, with a flash of insight, she knew exactly what love was. It was a man who didn't believe in it risking his heart by asking her to marry him. It was a man who couldn't find the words showing her over and over again with his steadfastness and tenderness that he loved her. It was a man who hadn't gone away because she'd said no, but instead had stayed, proving his love with his presence and commitment. It was a man who trusted her enough to ask her to become the mother of the daughter he adored.

Hands shaking and heart pounding, she walked outside and knelt in the dirt beside him. He glanced at her, his eyes filled with desire and shadowed by questions.

"Yes," she said quietly, praying that single word would be enough. Like him, she wasn't sure she knew what else to say to make things right, to grab forever.

He gave her a puzzled look. "Yes?"

Her lips curved. "Have you forgotten the question?"

After an eternity, hope suddenly shone in his eyes. "How could I?" he asked simply. "It's the most important one I've ever asked.'' He searched her face. ''Are you sure?''

''That I love you? Yes. Without question.''

''Enough to stay here?''

''Yes.''

''What about the rest?'' he asked. ''Do you know how I feel?''

Even now he was leaving it to her to figure things out, but she no longer minded. The truth was in his eyes. ''About you loving me? I know that, too. Someday you'll see the feelings for what they are, and then you'll say the words. I can wait. I just can't wait alone.''

He nodded slowly. ''I was thinking a summer wedding,'' he said, reaching into his pocket.

His tone was nonchalant, but Melanie could see the vulnerability in his eyes. He still wasn't sure of her, wasn't sure of any of this, but he was taking a gigantic leap of faith for her, for both of them.

''The garden should be in shape by then,'' he continued as he withdrew a velvet jeweler's box and held it out. ''What do you think?''

Melanie took the box with shaking hands and opened it. The diamond inside sparkled like the sun. She grinned. ''Is that why you've been working so hard out here?''

He gave her a chagrined look. ''I guess subconsciously I was hoping you'd change your mind.''

''And if I hadn't?''

''Then I would have found the words,'' he said confidently. ''They're in my heart, Melanie.'' He pressed her hand to his chest. ''Can you feel them with each beat?''

She smiled at him. ''Steady and enduring,'' she said at once. ''They're good words, Mike.''

"And love?" he asked quietly. "You didn't feel that?"

She lifted her gaze to his. "It's in your eyes," she told him. "In your touch. In everything you do."

He sighed. "As long as you know," he said.

He took the ring and slipped it on her finger. It was a perfect fit. *They* were a perfect fit.

"I'm sorry I ever doubted it," she said.

"Maybe we both have to learn to have more faith," he said quietly. "We've been given a gift. We simply have to nurture it."

Her eyes stinging with tears, Melanie glanced around at the profusion of flowers that had come from this man's nurturing touch. Love was blooming everywhere. "I think you're just the man to show me the way."

Epilogue

Colleen D'Angelo stood at the back door of Rose Cottage, staring out at the garden, tears in her eyes. Melanie regarded her mother worriedly.

"Mom, are you okay?"

"I'm speechless," she said, her voice barely above a whisper. "It's beautiful, just the way it was when your grandmother was alive. How on earth did you remember it so clearly? I'd forgotten."

"I didn't," Melanie admitted. "I showed Mike a picture, and he knew exactly what to do. It's almost as if he felt some sort of connection with grandmother. He fussed and badgered until I agreed to let him put the garden back the way it had been."

"He's a wonderful man, this Mike of yours," her mother said, smiling at her. "He's making you happy?"

"Of course," Melanie said, laughing. "We're getting married in an hour."

"That's more than enough time to change your mind," her mother informed her. "I can't believe you want to move here. You've always been such a city girl."

"Mike's here," Melanie said simply. "And when we get back from our honeymoon, I'm going to open my own marketing firm. Mike will be my first client. Not that I want him working any harder than he already does, but he won't be nearly as demanding as other clients might be. He'll forgive my mistakes while I'm learning the ropes. And Jeff and Pam want me to put together a marketing proposal for the nursery. Starting out with two clients isn't bad."

Her mother gave her a fierce hug. "I'm so happy for you. Your father's fit to be tied that you're not coming home. Don't be surprised if he punches Mike in the nose for taking you away from us, instead of giving the bride away the way he's supposed to."

Melanie stared at her with alarm. "Dad wouldn't really do that, would he?" She asked because it wasn't beyond the realm of possibility. He was a very protective dad, and he'd been regarding Mike with suspicion ever since they'd arrived for the wedding.

"Not as long as Mike keeps you smiling," her mother assured her.

"That won't be a problem," Melanie said, just as her sisters burst into the kitchen.

"Hey, why are you two standing down here in your robes crying? We have a wedding in less than an hour," Ashley announced.

"I think they're having the *S-E-X* talk," Jo teased.

"Ah, that must be it," Maggie chimed in. "See how flushed Melanie's cheeks are."

"Stop it, girls," their mother ordered in the no-nonsense tone they'd learned early to obey.

"Yes, ma'am," they chorused, then burst into giggles.

Melanie grinned at them. They'd laughed more in the past twenty-four hours than they had in years. She was going to miss them desperately.

Maybe she'd just have to figure out some way to lure them to Virginia. Surely the magic of Rose Cottage hadn't been used up on her and Mike.

"Daddy, stop wiggling," Jessie said, her expression solemn as she surveyed him. "You look gorgeous." She twirled around. "How do I look?"

"Like a fairy princess," Mike said, his heart in his throat. Melanie's insistence that Jessie give him away, rather than taking the more traditional flower-girl role, had been just right. Jessie was taking her responsibility very seriously. Jeff had hardly anything left to do in his capacity as best man.

"I'm feeling extraneous," he grumbled, running a finger under the collar of his shirt. "Tell me again why I'm wearing a tux, when I could have been sitting in the crowd in a suit?"

"You're the best man," Jessie told him. "But I'm more important."

Jeff laughed as Mike scooped Jessie into his arms. "You are indeed, short stuff. Now let's get this show on the road."

The three of them took their places in the garden as the organ music began. Mike's gaze locked on the back door of the house, where first one D'Angelo sister emerged and then the next. They were all beautiful in their rose-colored gowns, but there was only one sister he was desperate to see.

Then Melanie emerged in a slim gown of white silk and lace, a bouquet of white roses and lily of the valley from the garden in her hands. Her gaze locked with his, and a radiant smile blossomed on her face. It was a stark contrast to the glower on her father's features. Max D'Angelo didn't scare Mike. He knew the man wanted only the best for his daughter, and Mike intended to exceed his expectations. He had a hunch he'd be just as fiercely protective when Jessie found the man of her dreams—say, thirty years from now.

When Melanie reached Mike's side, the minister asked, "Who gives this couple to be wed?"

Max D'Angelo glanced down at Jessie standing solemnly by his side and tucked her tiny hand in his. "We do," they said together.

"My love for you will be eternal," Mike said when the time came, clearly taking Melanie by surprise with vows he'd labored to write himself. "Like this garden, it will have cycles, but it will always bloom and thrive. It will weather every storm and reach for the sunlight. If we nurture it, our joy will be bountiful."

"Oh, Mike," she whispered, looking as if she might weep.

"Don't you dare cry," he said. "Or I'll never say anything romantic again."

She laughed at that, and the world righted itself. He sighed, gazing into her sparkling eyes. This was it, he thought. This was love—looking into Melanie's eyes and finding that his world was complete.

"I thought I was the one who had all the words," Melanie said slowly. "But you've left me speechless, Mike. 'I love you' doesn't seem to be nearly enough, and yet it's everything. I love you and your daughter. I love the family we will become, the children we will have somewhere along the way. I love that you've taken me into your heart, and I promise you will always be in mine.''

Mike grinned at her. ''Not so speechless, after all.''

The minister cleared his throat. ''My turn?'' he inquired.

''Absolutely,'' they both said.

''Then I now pronounce you husband and wife.'' He gazed out at the crowd. ''Ladies and gentlemen, I present Mr. and Mrs. Mikelewski.''

Jessie tugged on the minister's clerical robe. ''What about me?'' she asked, drawing laughter.

''And daughter,'' the minister said.

Mike was about to reach for Jessie, but Melanie was there first, scooping her new daughter up in her arms, then reaching for Mike's hand. Together the three of them walked down the aisle.

A family, he thought happily. The way it should be. The way it would *always* be.

* * * * *

And now, turn the page for a sneak
preview of Maggie D'Angelo's story,
WHAT'S COOKING?,
the second book in Sherryl Woods's
exciting new series,
ROSE COTTAGE SISTERS.
On sale in April 2005
from Silhouette Special Edition.

Prologue

She was apparently addicted to sex. That was the only conclusion Margaret D'Angelo could come up with to explain this ridiculous habit she had of convincing herself she was wildly in love with a man she barely knew. She'd made way too many bad choices in her twenty-seven years based on letting her hormones overrule her head. She was not about to make another one.

And when it came to photographer Rick Flannery, he all but had the phrase *bad choice* tattooed on his forehead. It didn't take a genius to figure that one out. The man was a talented world-renowned fashion photographer. That Maggie had even met him was such a fluke, she could still hardly believe it. Under normal circumstances, their paths would never cross. She set up photo shoots of *food*, for goodness' sake! The most glamorous things on her magazine's pages wore decadent icing, not makeup.

Rick had merely stepped in at the last minute to do a favor for a friend. She figured that was about the most luck she could count on where he was concerned.

To add to her conviction that any relationship was doomed, she recognized that he was surrounded daily by some of the most gorgeous women in the world. The tabloids carried a picture of him almost every week with yet another model on his arm. Society columns linked his name with women from around the globe. Rarely was it the same name twice. That did not bode well for her own relationship with him.

Yes, indeed, for once in her life Maggie actually got it *before* she made the kind of mistake she'd live to regret, *before* she confused passionate sex with eternal love. Just this once she was going to sever all ties with a man *before* he could break her heart. This sane, rational thought might not have come to her in time to keep her from sleeping with Rick, but it sure as hell was in time to keep her from falling for him.

Proud of herself for making such a calm, intelligent decision for once and backing it up with a plan of action, she marched into her big sister's law office in a prestigious Boston skyscraper and held out her hand. "Give me the key," she demanded grimly.

Ashley's head snapped up from the stack of paperwork on her cluttered desk. She stared at Maggie blankly. Clearly her mind was still on whatever high-profile case she was preparing to take to court.

"What key?" Ashley asked, sounding surprisingly less quick-witted than she did when she was defending one of her clients against an aggressive prosecutor.

"To Rose Cottage, dammit!" Their grandmother's

cottage was far away from Boston. Rick knew absolutely nothing about it. Maggie figured she could hide out there until this attraction or whatever it was cooled down, until it became nothing more than a distant memory. Down there in the boonies, she might not even have to see his picture in some tabloid with whatever model *du jour* was taking her place. That was definitely án added bonus.

"Why?" Ashley asked.

"I'm taking a vacation, that's why," Maggie retorted.

Ashley looked even more surprised. Maggie was no more in the habit of taking time off than Ashley was. She might not maintain Ashley's workaholic pace, but she didn't like being too far from the office and the whirlwind that publishing a monthly magazine entailed.

"Sit," Ashley commanded, waiting patiently until Maggie relented and complied. "What's going on, Maggie?"

"Rick Flannery is going on," Maggie responded, blurting out the words without thinking of the consequences. Ashley went into full protective big-sister mode. It was an awesome, sometimes intimidating transformation, especially for the person on the receiving end of her wrath.

"The photographer?" Ashley asked, getting a better grip on her pen and looking as if she might start taking notes and readying some sort of suit against the man at any second if she didn't find Maggie's answers satisfactory. "The one you've been raving about ever since he stepped in at the last minute to do the photo shoot for the July issue of your magazine? The one who could make the most ordinary mac and cheese look like gourmet fare, even though he normally takes pretty pictures of gorgeous women? The man who has eyes as crystal blue as a lake and a tight little butt? *That* Rick Flannery?''

"Yes, that Rick Flannery," Maggie snapped. As if there could possibly be another one, she thought irritably. Wasn't it bad enough that there was one of him? And did her sister have to remember every blasted thing she'd ever said about the man?

To Maggie's shock, Ashley leaned back and grinned. "The man's got your hormones all stirred up, hasn't he? Why didn't I see that the first time you mentioned his name? When you started waxing eloquent about his body, it should have been a dead giveaway."

Maggie remained stubbornly silent.

"So?" Ashley prodded. "Does he make your heart pound and then some?"

"So what if he does? Nothing's going to come of it." Actually quite a lot had come of it, several glorious days and nights of unbridled passion, in fact. That was the problem, but Ashley didn't need to know it. Nor was Maggie about to add that he'd failed to call for six endless days now, pretty much proving her impression of a hit-and-run kind of a guy.

"Why not? Is there some reason the two of you can't be together?" Ashley persisted.

"Because he's Rick Flannery, dammit! There are a hundred—no, maybe a thousand—absolutely gorgeous, willowy women who drool over him on a regular basis. I am not about to set myself up to compete with that." What they had might be very hot right now, but it wouldn't last, not with that kind of competition underfoot day in and day out. Maggie hadn't been able to sustain a relationship yet, not once the sex cooled down. And Rick, according to all sorts of tabloid accounts, was not known for ignoring temptation.

"You've already slept with him, haven't you?" Ashley inquired knowingly. "And it was fabulous. Otherwise you wouldn't be this scared."

Leave it to Ashley to see straight through her, Maggie thought with disgust. She'd hoped to get through this conversation with one tiny shred of dignity intact. Apparently that wasn't to be.

"Will you just give me the stupid key?" she grumbled.

"So you can hide out in grandmother's cottage until the attraction wears off?" Ashley surmised.

"Exactly."

"You do recall what happened when Melanie went there a few months ago, don't you? She was just as determined to avoid men as you are. One popped up anyway, and she's now married." There was a gloating note in Ashley's voice.

"A fluke. Lightning can't possibly strike twice," Maggie insisted. "That town is only so big. How many men can there possibly be like Melanie's Mike?"

Ashley chuckled. "It only takes one, sweetie." But even as she said it, she dug in her purse and retrieved the old-fashioned key that she kept there as some sort of bizarre talisman. She claimed it was a reminder to her that there was life outside the office. She held it out to Maggie. "Go. Enjoy."

"Thank you," Maggie said, grabbing the key and heading for the door.

"You're welcome. But when temptation comes calling, don't say I didn't warn you."

Maggie glared at her. "Bite your tongue."

Wasn't that the whole point of going into exile, after all? Temptation was going to be hundreds of miles away.

Following is a special sneak preview of
Sherryl Woods's 100th book
THE BACKUP PLAN.
On sale in March 2005
from MIRA books

Cord Beaufort lazily swatted at the fly circling his bottle of now-lukewarm beer. It was the end of a steamy, grueling day, a day that had tested his patience and sent his nerves into more of an uproar than the last time he'd engaged in far more pleasurable, rambunctious sex.

He'd had to meet with the board of directors for Covington Plantation. To a man—and woman—they were the most impossible, exasperating group of self-important human beings he'd ever had the misfortune to work for. They wanted to micromanage everything, and not a one of them had the expertise for it.

Worse, he'd had to wear a suit and tie, even though the temperature was pushing ninety. If there was one thing he hated more than placating a bunch of wealthy, egotistical bosses, it was wearing a damn suit and pretending not to be bored to tears while they yammered on and on. Things that should have been decided in an hour had taken the whole damn day.

Now he was stretched out in a well-used Pawleys Island hammock strung between two ancient live oaks, wearing jeans and nothing else, and trying his best not to move a muscle till a breeze stirred, which probably wouldn't happen till November. He was not feeling especially optimistic at the moment.

The sound of a car bouncing along the dirt lane leading to his house did nothing to improve his mood.

He wasn't feeling any more sociable than he was optimistic. That was one reason he'd left all the ruts in the damn road, to discourage visitors. Most people had long since gotten the message, which meant this had to be someone unexpected and probably troublesome.

When the car finally came into view, he tried to place it and couldn't. However, the sight of a pair of long, shapely bare legs emerging from the front seat did improve his outlook marginally. Only one woman in all of South Carolina had legs like that. Maybe only one woman on the face of the earth…and she pretty much hated his guts. To be honest, he couldn't say he blamed her.

If all the rumors he'd been hearing were right and Dinah Davis had decided to come home—and if she was on his doorstep—it could only mean one thing. She was here to claim his brother, Bobby, who'd made some idiotic promise to her years ago that he'd always be around if she ever decided to stop her globe-trotting and settle down with the common folks. Bobby, much as Cord loved him, was a damned fool. Who'd want a woman on terms like that, even a woman as drop-dead gorgeous as Dinah Davis?

Cord watched with fascination and masculine appreciation as she exited her car, wondering if her uppity mama knew she was going around town in a pair of shorts that left little to the imagination. That and her halter top, while appropriate for the weather, were not exactly on the approved fashion list for a one-time Charleston debutante who never strayed from the straight and narrow. Right now she looked more like somebody he wouldn't mind taking a tumble with, which would flat-out horrify her mama.

Then, again, maybe Dinah's choice of attire explained

why Mrs. Davis had been on such a royal tear at the board meeting today. A rebellious daughter, even one who was thirty-one or so by now and internationally famous, could do that to an uptight woman.

"Well, well," he murmured as Dinah lifted her chin with a familiar touch of defiance and started in his direction. "Just look at what the cat dragged in."

Bright patches of color immediately flooded her cheeks and those devastating, dark-blue eyes of hers flashed with irritation, but good breeding quickly kicked in. She was, after all, on his turf. An uninvited guest with manners, Cord thought with amusement as he awaited her response.

"Good evening, Cordell," she said, her voice as sweet as syrup, yet unmistakably insincere. "I see your manners haven't improved with age."

"Not much," he agreed, refusing to take offense. "Time's been kind to you, though. You're as pretty as Miss Scarlett and twice as tough, judging from what I've seen of you on TV."

"I'm amazed you watch network news," she said. "I thought the cartoon channel would be more to your liking."

"Sugar, I'm a man. Surfing channels is in my nature. Even I slow down when I see a hometown girl lighting up the screen in my living room, while bombs blow things up behind her."

"Yes, I imagine it gives you something to fantasize about on one of your lonely nights," she said, her voice cool with disdain.

"Sugar, I am never lonely except by choice." Lately, though, the truth was he was making that choice more and more. Women, gorgeous and fascinating though they could surely be, were proving to be more trouble than they were worth.

Dinah gave him a withering look obviously meant to convey the message that she found his claim laughable.

"As pleasant as it is chatting with you," she said in that same syrupy voice that was all about properly bred, South Carolina manners, "I'm here to see Bobby. Is he around?"

Cord took a long, slow sip of beer and an insolent, long, slow head-to-toe survey of her before replying. "Nope."

She regarded him with unmistakable impatience. "Expected back?"

Cord saw no reason to help her out when he disapproved so heartily of her apparent mission. "Eventually."

"Which means exactly what?"

He grinned. Riling Dinah had always been a snap. It was a pure pleasure to see that hadn't changed. "I thought I was clear enough. He'll be back when he gets back. You know how it goes with us lazy, good for nothing Beauforts. We're not much on timetables."

Dinah sighed heavily, which had a fascinating effect on the rise and fall of her barely clad breasts. Cord wondered if she had any notion at all of the raw sensuality she was projecting and just how close he was to summoning the energy to drag her straight into his arms for the kiss she was half-begging for. Probably not or she'd have hightailed it out of here, instead of pestering him for answers he had no intention of giving her. Come hell or high water, he intended to protect Bobby from his own foolishness.

"Is Bobby due back tonight? Tomorrow? Next week?" she asked, her tone impatient.

"Could be next week," he said, then shrugged. "Maybe not."

"Has anyone ever told you how impossible you are?"

"Before you?" he asked.

She scowled.

Cord grinned. "Now that you mention it, I believe your mama said something very similar to me just this afternoon."

Her eyes widened at that, pleasing Cord with the fact that he could still shock her. It had been one of his primary delights in life back when she and Bobby had been dating. It had been a long time since he'd taken such pleasure in stirring a woman's temper or her dismay.

"Where on earth did you see my mother?" she inquired.

Her tone came damn close to suggesting he surely must have done something illegal to have such an encounter with such an upper-crust paragon. If Dinah weren't so cute up there on her high horse, he might be insulted that she couldn't imagine any circumstance under which he and Dorothy Rawlings Davis would cross paths.

"Out and about," he replied mildly. "Charleston is, after all, a small town in many ways. In fact, I do believe that was why you were so anxious to leave."

"I left to attend college and pursue a career," she said, her voice tight as her cool gaze raked over him. "Maybe that's something you should consider doing."

He held up his beer and gestured around him. "Why leave? If you ask me, it doesn't get any better than this— a roof over my head, a little money in the bank, a cool drink and up until a few minutes ago plenty of peace and quiet."

"Thank heaven your brother doesn't share your total lack of ambition," she said.

She spoke in that uppity little voice that was starting to get on his nerves. He frowned at the comparison in which he came out wanting. He could have told her a few things about what he'd been up to, but why bother? She enjoyed thinking of him as a lowlife. Why take that pleasure away from her when she'd just gotten back to town?

"Please tell Bobby I'm home and looking forward to seeing him. You can remember a simple message, can't you?"

"If I put my mind to it," Cord agreed. Not that he intended to. Dinah Davis would eat his brother alive. Bobby didn't need the aggravation. Of course, the last time he'd tried thinking for his brother and interfering in his so-called romance with Dinah, there had been hell to pay.

"Well, try real hard," she said.

Then she sashayed back to her car, providing him with a fantastic view of her very fine derriere. Cord shook his head. Too bad she was so much trouble. Otherwise, he might enjoy tangling with her himself. Instead, he'd just content himself with keeping Bobby out of her clutches.

Silhouette®

SPECIAL EDITION™

GOLD RUSH GROOMS
Lucky in love—and striking it rich—
beneath the big skies of Montana!

The excitement of Montana Mavericks: GOLD RUSH GROOMS continues

with

PRESCRIPTION: LOVE
(SE #1669)

by favorite author

Pamela Toth

City slicker Zoe Hart hated doing her residency in a
one-horse town like Thunder Canyon. But each time
she passed handsome E.R. doctor Christopher Taylor in
the halls, her heart skipped a beat. And as they began
to spend time together, the sexy physician became a
temptation Zoe wasn't sure she wanted to give up. When
faced with a tough professional choice, would Zoe opt to
go back to city life—or stay in Thunder Canyon with the
man who made her pulse race like no other?

Available at your favorite retail outlet.

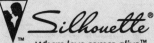

Silhouette®

Where love comes alive™

SPECIAL EDITION™

Don't miss the second installment in the
exciting new continuity, beginning in
Silhouette Special Edition.

THE FORTUNES OF TEXAS: Reunion

A TYCOON IN TEXAS

by Crystal Green

Available March 2005

Silhouette Special Edition #1670

Christina Mendoza couldn't help being attracted
to her new boss, Derek Rockwell. But as she
knew from experience, it was best to keep things
professional. Working in close quarters only
heightened the attraction, though, and when family
started to interfere would Christina find the courage
to claim her love?

**Fortunes of Texas: Reunion—
The power of family.**

Available at your favorite retail outlet.

Silhouette®
Where love comes alive™

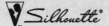

SPECIAL EDITION™

Introducing a brand-new miniseries by
Silhouette Special Edition favorite author
Marie Ferrarella

One special necklace,
three charm-filled romances!

BECAUSE A HUSBAND
IS FOREVER

by Marie Ferrarella

Available March 2005
Silhouette Special Edition #1671

Dakota Delany had always wanted a marriage like
the one her parents had, but after she found her
fiancé cheating, she gave up on love. When her
radio talk show came up with the idea of having her
spend two weeks with hunky bodyguard Ian Russell,
she protested—until she discovered she wanted Ian
to continue guarding her body forever!

Available at your favorite retail outlet.

Where love comes alive™

If you enjoyed what you just read,
then we've got an offer you can't resist!

Take 2 bestselling love stories FREE!

Plus get a FREE surprise gift!

Clip this page and mail it to Silhouette Reader Service™

IN U.S.A.	IN CANADA
3010 Walden Ave.	P.O. Box 609
P.O. Box 1867	Fort Erie, Ontario
Buffalo, N.Y. 14240-1867	L2A 5X3

YES! Please send me 2 free Silhouette Special Edition® novels and my free surprise gift. After receiving them, if I don't wish to receive anymore, I can return the shipping statement marked cancel. If I don't cancel, I will receive 6 brand-new novels every month, before they're available in stores! In the U.S.A., bill me at the bargain price of $4.24 plus 25¢ shipping and handling per book and applicable sales tax, if any*. In Canada, bill me at the bargain price of $4.99 plus 25¢ shipping and handling per book and applicable taxes**. That's the complete price and a savings of at least 10% off the cover prices—what a great deal! I understand that accepting the 2 free books and gift places me under no obligation ever to buy any books. I can always return a shipment and cancel at any time. Even if I never buy another book from Silhouette, the 2 free books and gift are mine to keep forever.

235 SDN DZ9D
335 SDN DZ9E

Name	(PLEASE PRINT)	
Address	Apt.#	
City	State/Prov.	Zip/Postal Code

Not valid to current Silhouette Special Edition® subscribers.

Want to try two free books from another series?
Call 1-800-873-8635 or visit www.morefreebooks.com.

* Terms and prices subject to change without notice. Sales tax applicable in N.Y.
** Canadian residents will be charged applicable provincial taxes and GST.
All orders subject to approval. Offer limited to one per household.
® are registered trademarks owned and used by the trademark owner and its licensee.

SPED04R   ©2004 Harlequin Enterprises Limited

e♦HARLEQUIN.com

The Ultimate Destination for Women's Fiction

Becoming an eHarlequin.com member is easy, fun and **FREE!** Join today to enjoy great benefits:

- **Super savings** on all our books, including members-only discounts and offers!

- Enjoy **exclusive online reads**—FREE!

- Info, tips and **expert advice** on writing your own romance novel.

- FREE romance **newsletters,** customized by you!

- Find out the latest on your **favorite authors.**

- Enter to win exciting **contests and promotions!**

- Chat with other members in our **community message boards!**

To become a member,
visit www.eHarlequin.com today!

INTMEMB04R

Curl up and have a

Heart *to* Heart

with

Harlequin Romance®

Just like having a heart-to-heart
with your best friend, these stories
will take you from laughter to tears
and back again. So heartwarming
and emotional you'll want to
have some tissues handy!

Next month Harlequin is thrilled to bring you
Natasha Oakley's first book for Harlequin Romance:

For Our Children's Sake (#3838),
on sale March 2005

Then watch out for....

A Family For Keeps (#3843),
by Lucy Gordon, on sale May 2005

Available wherever Harlequin books are sold.

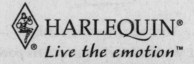

HARLEQUIN®
Live the emotion™

www.eHarlequin.com   HRHTH